CATCHING LIGHTNING BUGS IN A JAR

2024 KWA Anthology

Brian Balzer
Sonny Collins
Starla Criser
Jana Dahmen
Jerry J. Fanning
Mike Freed
Duane L Herrmann
Katherine Pritchett
Elie Stone
Laura Wright

ISBN: 9798339026280

Cover design - **MIKE FREED**

Editor - **SONNY COLLINS**

Prairie Moon Publications

The Kansas Writers Association (KWA)
Is a non-profit organization
That encourages, inspires and teaches
Writers of all genres
To do their very best.

KWA Anthologies

The Big and Small of Us All - 2013
When Words Bloom - 2014
By Invitation Only - 2015
Kansas Dreams - 2016
Words That Flow - 2017
Taking Turns Telling Tales - 2018
Thoughts Yet to Tell - 2019
Words From Other Voices - 2021
Writers & Werewolves - 2022
Tales Told Well - 2023

5

THE VERDICT
Brian Balzer

Hank sat sipping coffee while gazing at a smattering of familiar faces in the only café of the small town he'd grown up in. He knew most by name, although he couldn't remember the names of some of the younger folks right at that moment.

His best friend, Rick, sat across from him staring idly out the café window for no particular reason at the cars passing by on Main Street. He glanced at Hank's newspaper and then back out the window at the passing cars.

They'd been having breakfast together at the café for decades. Both of them still remembered the day it opened. They'd seen it change hands twice, and remodeled three times.

Hank gave the young waitress, Tishona, a nod when she glanced at him. She knew he was ready for a refill without asking. Soon she was topping off their cups with piping hot coffee.

"Thanks," they said simply before she turned and walked away without a response. They knew she was having a rough morning so neither of them took it personal.

While Rick returned his gaze out the window, Hank looked around briefly once more, and unrolled his morning paper.

The front page headline jumped out at him – Trial Postponed. He began skimming the article. 'Local man facing trial… Trial once again postponed… unable to stand trial at this time… listed in critical condition…'

"Order up!" Bruce called out from the order window.

Without looking Hank knew it was too soon for it to be his breakfast. Although he'd tried everything they served dozens of times, Hank had once again ordered sausage links, eggs, and pancakes, which he favored over everything else.

"Read this yet?" Hank asked Rick nonchalantly.

"Ya know I haven't," Rick replied while glancing at the paper.

"Got it put off again," Hank stated matter-of-factly.

Rick sipped his coffee. "Did that already didn't they?"

"Twice," Hank murmured as he reached for his cup. "That slick city lawyer a his asked fer more time ta prepare first time, then jus' happen ta be down with the flu the second time it wus 'sposed ta go ta trial."

Rick lowered his cup. "Whut'd they put it off fer this time?"

"He's laid up in the hospital in rough condition accordin' ta the paper," Hank answered, nodding at his paper.

"Order up!" Bruce called out once again.

"The lawyer?" Rick questioned.

Hank shook his head. "Ole Chester is."

"How come?" Rick pried for information.

"Got beat within an inch'v his life," Hank answered as he laid his paper down.

"Jus' goes ta show that ev'ry inch counts," Rick stated casually just before Tishona brought them their plates.

***

Hank sipped his hot coffee while watching the dark clouds hanging in the sky. *'Wonder if it'll break loose er if I'll hafta water the garden later.'*

Rick had called and asked Hank to order scrambled eggs and toast for him. Hank had decided on French toast, sausage patties, and eggs over easy for himself.

He was reading an article stating that the man who

had been severely beaten a few months prior was scheduled to appear in court the following week.

'Reckon we'll know soon,' Hank thought just before a shrill cry rang out over the clammer of voices in the café.

Hank shot a look of sympathy to the young woman whose toddler had suddenly decided to begin screaming. Seconds later the toddler melted into the floor as Hank turned his hearing-aid down.

'Times like this I'm glad I'm deaf in one ear an can barely hear outta the other,' he thought as the toddler screamed until she was red in the face.

Tishona knelt down beside the crying child. "What's wrong Susie?" she asked, hoping to defuse the situation for the frazzled young mother, as well as everyone else in the café.

Susie's mother sighed tiredly while her child cried harder. "She's done decided her toast's burnt."

"Well, let me fix that!" Tishona declared as she stood up. "Fresh toast, coming right up!" she announced as she reached for a saucer with a medium toasted piece of bread on it.

Susie quieted almost instantly as Tishona turned on her heel. She laid in the floor for a moment longer sniffling as she watched Tishona disappear through a swinging door. She was just getting back into her booster seat when Tishona returned.

"How does that look?" Tishona asked as she sat the saucer with the same slice of toast in front of the toddler. "Better?"

Susie glanced at the toast, sniffled once more, and nodded.

"Thanks," Chelsey sighed gratefully. "Ya might jus' be the best waitress they ever had workin' here."

Tishona smiled and blushed slightly. "We all have those

days," she assured her gently. "I've had adults do the same thing," she whispered with a wink.

"Order up!" Bruce's voice rang out loudly.

Marilyn, an older woman dining alone at the next table over, glared at Tishona. *'I Know you were talking about me!'* Luckily Tishona was already past her table before she could think of anything scornful to say.

"Here you go Ms. Roedel," Tishona said politely a minute later as she sat Marilyn's flapjacks on the table in front of her. "Enjoy your breakfast."

"I intend to!" Marilyn blurted when she couldn't think of anything snarky to say. She wanted to demand that Tishona bring her something else, however, the exceptional young waitress had already provided everything she could possibly need for her meal.

"Good morning. You timed it perfectly," Tishona told Rick who entered the café as she was headed towards the table where Hank sat.

"G'mornin'," Rick greeted her politely as she placed his plate on the table across from Hank.

Tishona was placing Hank's breakfast in front of him as he was reaching for his hearing-aid. When Hank held up a finger while turning his hearing-aid back up she waited until after he'd lowered his hand to say, "Here you go Sir. Will there be anything else?"

"Young lady, ya know callin' me 'Sir' is like puttin' curtains in an outhouse," Hank replied with a soft chuckle.

"Yes Sir. I do Sir," Tishona agreed with a twinkle in her eyes. "I happen to like a fancy outhouse though Sir. Nice curtains on the window, a little chandelier, a decorative paper holder..."

Hank found himself grinning a bit wider than he had been before. "I guess, if ya say so."

"I do say so," Tishona told him kindly. "Would you

like anything else to go with your meal other than your coffee?" she asked Rick with a smile.

"Not right off," Rick replied as he scooted up to the table.

"I'll be right back with your coffee," Tishona informed him.

"I like that lil gal," Rick said with a grin, "but she shore has a funny way a talkin'."

"Can't say as yer wrong 'bout that," Hank told him while folding his paper shut.

***

A week later Hank sat in the same chair at the same table. He glanced up from his newspaper when a bell over the front door jingled. "Here comes trouble!"

Rick grinned in response. "Ya know it!" Just as he was passing behind ten year old Brady, the boy leaned his chair backwards onto its back legs. Rick paused long enough to push the chair forward, startling Brady. "Got more'n two legs fer a reason boy!"

"Yes Sir," Brady responded sheepishly while his mother smiled up at Rick.

"Mornin' Rick," Sheila said sweetly.

"Mornin' Miss Reed," Rick replied politely. "Mind if I join ya?" he directed his question towards Hank as he approached his table.

"Reckon ya could," Hank answered as he laid his paper on the table. He pushed the other chair out with his foot just before Rick took hold of it.

"Couldn't wait huh?" Rick asked with a nod towards Hank's plate.

"Nope, stomach wuseatin' my backbone," Hank replied while salting his eggs.

"So, whut's the news?" Rick questioned with a glance at the newspaper.

"Ole Chester's lawyer got it put off again," Hank

answered as he drizzled syrup over his pancakes and eggs.

"Whut's the excuse this time?" Rick asked as he turned a coffee cup over and sat it on its saucer.

"Pri-or ob-luh-gation," Hank drew out his answer while cutting a bite of pancakes to stuff into his mouth. "Lawyer's got a case bein' tried in another state," he answered the question Rick was about to ask.

Rick scratched an itch on his neck. "How much time'd it buy 'im?"

"Month an a half," Hank replied after swallowing. "Lucky he got any."

"Uh huh," Rick murmured as Tishona approached their table.

"Good morning Sir," she said politely while filling Rick's coffee cup.

"Ha!" Hank blurted around a bite of extra crispy bacon. "Callin' HIM Sir is even MORE like puttin' curtains in an outhouse!"

"Hey! I ruhzemble that remark!" Rick erupted with a laugh.

Tishona rolled her eyes and giggled. "What can I bring you?"

"Food!" Rick declared with a snicker.

"One plate of beets coming right up!" Tishona replied with a smirk while pretending to write it down.

"Hey now," Rick said with a frown. "No need ta be mean."

Tishona pretended to scratch the imaginary order off of her pad. "What will it be instead?"

"Uh... Western omelet, toast, an a side'v bacon," Rick answered decisively.

"Got it," Tishona noted before turning on her heel.

"Hey Tish, don't ferget ta tell Bruce not ta burn my bacon like he does Hank's," Rick needled with a grin.

Tishona headed for the order window without replying. She knew that Rick just wanted to give Hank a hard time.

"Ain't burnt," Hank stated as he broke one of his over easy yolks with a piece of bacon. "Not my fault ya like yers raw."

"Don't like it raw," Rick retorted before taking a sip of his coffee. "Jus' don't like it overcooked."

Hank took a bite of bacon with yolk dripping from it. "Uh huh, if it bends without breakin', might as well be raw."

"Mind if I read yer paper?" Rick asked as Hank cut a bite of egg.

"Ya been comin' in here an readin' my paper fer years," Hank pointed out while stabbing a bite of pancake to go with the egg. "Why would I all a sudden mind now?"

"Are ya finished with it?" Rick asked without answering the question even though he knew that Hank probably wasn't done with his paper.

"No," Hank mumbled around the bite, "but ya can read on it 'til I'm ready ta take it back."

"Fair 'nough," Rick agreed with a nod before taking another sip of coffee. "Mmm… good coffee."

"Always is," Hank pointed out before taking a sip of his own coffee.

"Mhm," Rick hummed as he opened the paper.

The two sat in silence while Hank ate his breakfast and Rick read the paper. Just as Hank was finishing up his meal Tishona brought Rick's food to their table.

"Ready for more coffee?" she asked as she put Rick's plate in front of him.

"Whenever it's conven'yent," Hank answered as he handed her his empty plate.

"It's convenient whenever you're ready," Tishona

countered with a smile. "Need anything besides more coffee?"

Hank nodded slightly, "Yeah, some toast an jelly. Didn't quite get filled up."

"I'll get you some," Tishona replied with a nod. She then giggled softly, "Just don't throw a tantrum if it's not toasted Perfectly," she all but whispered.

"No promises," Hank replied with a wink.

***

The month and a half hadn't quite passed when another article announced another continuance. It was no longer front page news and had been shifted to page three.

"So the sorry son'v a gun got Another three months," Rick said while shaking his head. "Wuzn't his lawyer sick last time it wuz'sposed ta go ta trial?"

"Thinkin' thatwuza time er two buhfore," Hank noted as Tishona headed towards them with a pot of hot coffee. He sat his cup on its saucer and slid it towards the side of the table. "Last time Ole Chester's lawyer hada pri-or ob-luh-gation. Time buhfore that Ole Chesterwuz laid up in the hospital."

"Oh, right," Rick murmured as he did the same with his cup. He handed Hank's paper back as Tishona was walking away after taking their orders. "Why'd they put it off this time?"

"Ain't sure. Article didn't say nothin' 'bout it, but I'd heard his lawyer wuzgonna try an get it moved a couple counties over," Hank informed Rick quietly.

"That right?" Rick asked after swallowing.

"It's whut I'd heard," Hank told him matter-of-factly.

"Good morning," Tishona said when the bell over the door jingled. "Have a seat anywhere. I'll be right with you."

Debbie directed her husband towards a booth. "Let's

take a booth."

"Works fer me," her husband replied.

"Whut's the excuse fertryin' ta move it?" Rick asked after a sip of coffee.

"Claimed he woodn't get a fair trial 'round here 'cause too many folks're upset 'bout why he's a facin' trialta begin with," Hank answered before getting a sip.

"Woodn't matter," Rick stated, inhaling the aroma of bacon. "Word travels 'tween kinfolk faster'n light, an kinfolk 'round here're spread out lots more'n three counties in ev'ryd'rection."

"Ya got that right," Hank agreed with a nod.

"Think the judge'll allow it?" Rick asked after a moment of silence.

"Nope," Hank answered without hesitation. "Won't get it put off much more neither. Judge Booker's gettin' fed up with Ole Chester's lawyer."

"Su'prised they got whut they did," Rick commented while glancing about. "That slick city lawyer Ole Chester hired thought he wuz smart ta ask fer a jury trial 'stead'v a bench trial."

"Don't think it'll matter much," Hank pointed out.

"Think his goose's cooked?" Rick asked with a gleam in his eyes.

"Think his goose's been in a boilin' pot since he got arrested fer it," Hank declared evenly. "Jus' a matter of it bein' declared done."

"Su'prised it ain't boiled over yet," Rick stated while eyeing someone's omelet.

"Mhm," Hank hummed his response before sipping his coffee.

The two men made small talk until Tishona brought their breakfast then a comfortable silence fell between them while they ate their food and Hank read his paper.

"Anythin' new over in yer neck a the woods?" Rick

asked after they'd finished eating.

"Ya hear Bart fell off his wagon?" Hank asked as he picked up his coffee.

"Hadn't heard it," Rick answered simply.

"Mhm, 'parently his mule shied," Hank informed him after a sip.

"That right?" Rick muttered with a chortle.

"Jumped near a foot an Bart fell off his wagon onta his head," Hank said with a glint in his eyes.

Rick chuckled softly, "Least he landed on somethin' he couldn't hurt."

"Lucky fer him the ole gal didn't run a mile like last time," Hank pointed out with a grin.

"Or more," Rick said with a laugh. "Only stopped last time 'cause she got hung up." Just as he was about to turn and wave Tishona down, she walked up beside him. "If yawuz any better a waitress they'd have ta fire ya."

"Oh hush," Tishona said with a slight blush. She refilled their coffee cups, picked up their plates, then asked, "Anything else?"

"Whutkinda pie ya got?" Rick asked in return.

"Apple, cherry, blueberry," Tishona answered without looking towards the pie savers.

"No coconut cream?" Rick asked disappointedly.

"I'm afraid not," Tishona responded kindly.

"Reminds me'v a joke," Rick said with a grin.

"Don't tell it," Hank asserted pointedly.

"I've heard it," Tishona proclaimed with a giggle.

"Now how'd'ya know that?" Rick asked while pretending to be slightly hurt.

"We heard all yer jokes," Hank accused coolly.

"Twice," Tishona professed with a grin. "You want pie?"

Rick sighed softly, "Yeah, fetch me somethin' in a

bit."

"Which kind?" Tishona asked with a raised eyebrow.

"Don't matter," Rick declared, "you pick."

"Blueberry?" Tishona questioned.

"Don't matter if'n it ain't coconut cream," Rick avowed dejectedly.

"Fetch us each one a whichever ya got the most'v," Hank suggested before getting a sip of coffee.

"Blueberry," Tishona said with a shrug.

"It'll be fine," Hank told her as the bell over the door jingled again.

"No rush," Rick pointed out. "Jus' whenever."

"Thanks," Tishona said sweetly. "Take a seat wherever you'd like. I'll be Right with you!" she announced to the newcomers.

"Are yagonna work the crossword?" Rick asked while eyeing Hank's paper.

"Always do," Hank retorted.

"Need any help?" Rick asked with a grin.

"Never do," Hank declared, setting his cup down. "Guess I could let ya pretend ta help."

"HA! I'm better at 'em," Rick countered in response.

"Uh huh," Hank murmured as he turned to the crossword. "Shhureya are."

"Glad we agree!" Rick retorted with a smirk.

By the time the two of them had finished the crossword puzzle, they had also finished their pie, as well as an entire pot of coffee between the two of them.

***

"Mornin'," Bruce greeted as he unlocked the café door.

Hank yawned. "Mornin'."

"Yer here awful early," Bruce commented as he opened the door. "Hope yer not starvin'."

"Nah, jus' couldn't sleep," Hank all but grumbled.

"Woke up 'round three. Laid there hopin' ta fall back ta sleep fer a couple a hours an jus' fin'lly gave up."

"Well, come on in an I'll get a pot brewin'," Bruce suggested.

"Thanks," Hank murmured.

"Be awhile buhfore I'll be ready ta cook," Bruce informed him as they went inside. "Gotta do Night Cook's prep work."

"Coffee's fine fer now," Hank told him as he headed for his usual small round table. "Not all that hungry yet anyhow."

"That makes one'v us," Bruce admitted with a slight groan. "Overslept. Hadta skip breakfast."

"Fix yerselfsomethin' first chance ya get," Hank suggested while stifling a yawn.

"Not really 'sposed ta do that," Bruce told him with a sigh. "Hardly wait 'till the coffee's ready though."

Hank studied Bruce for a moment as he got a pot of coffee brewing. "Tell yawhut, decide whut sounds good an fix it fer me. Not yer fault if I change my mind."

"Well…" Bruce debated while looking at the empty parking spots.

"No one'll ever know an I'll pay fer it," Hank stated evenly. "Fer cryin' out loud. Yer only human man. Ya ain't no Saint. Ya need food."

"I'on't know," Bruce struggled with his conscience.

Hank narrowed his eyes. "If ya don't I'll stop eatin' here."

"That's a idle threat anya know it," Bruce declared with a grin.

Hank shrugged and pulled out a chair. "Let's not find out."

"Hey! I got plenty a Belgian waffle batter!" Bruce remembered excitedly. "Woodn't take much ta heat up the waffle maker."

"Sounds good," Hank admitted even though he really wasn't all that hungry.

"Run one out ferya in a bit if ya pour us some coffee when it's ready," Bruce suggested as the aroma of coffee filled the air.

Hank yawned again. "Uh huh, bet on that."

Without another word Bruce disappeared through the swinging door to the kitchen. "DAGNABIT!" he shouted over a loud clatter of pots and pans. "Night Cook don't learn ta put stuff away after closin' an Immawhoop'im!"

"From whut I've heard I'da already whooped'im!" Hank hollered back into the kitchen with a chuckle.

"Whooped who?" Tishona asked from the front door as the bell jingled.

"NIGHT COOK!" Bruce yelled from the kitchen.

"What did he do this time?" Tishona asked as she crossed the café.

"Left a stacka pots 'n pans in the floor at the end'v the prep table!" Bruce hollered angrily.

"Has he had his coffee yet?" Tishona asked in a hushed voice.

Hank shook his head before glancing at the little bit of coffee in the pot. "Thinkin' he needs it more'n I do."

Tishona pulled two cups out of a rack and placed one on the counter next to the coffee maker. She then held the other one under the dripping coffee while pouring the half cup's worth out into the cup on the counter. "This will help."

She took the half-filled coffee cup to Bruce who was angrily gathering up scattered pots and pans. "Here, have a few sips. I'll get the rest."

"Not yer job," Bruce grumbled as he shoved a small stack of pots underneath the prep table. 'Bad 'nough he didn't get prep done!"

"It's not yours either," Tishona pointed out. "Let's get it done together... After you've had a few sips of coffee."

"Fine," Bruce grumbled as he took the cup. While he took a few sips of the hot coffee he watched Tishona corral several pots with her foot before bending over to pick them up. "Thanks," he mumbled after a few more sips.

"You're welcome," Tishona replied kindly.

"Already buhind schedule," Bruce said with a sigh.

"Corina closed last night so the front end is in really good shape," Tishona told him as she worked the pots under the prep table. "What can I help you with?"

"Well, ya could tickle the shredded cheese," Bruce stated evenly.

"Are you being serious?" Tishona asked with a raised eyebrow.

"Well, yeah," Bruce answered after another sip of coffee. "Means loosenin' it up. Clumps tagether in the walk-in. Ya really kinda tickle it with yer fingertips."

"Ok, show me," Tishona conceded while picking up the last pan from the floor.

Soon they were each doing prep work while the Belgian waffle maker heated up. By the time Tishona had a bag of shredded cheese loosened up and ready to use, Bruce was pulling the first golden brown Belgian waffle out of the waffle maker.

"What's next?" Tishona asked when she saw he was putting more batter into the waffle maker.

"Take it ta the walk-in an grab a box'v sliced cheese from the shelfbuhneath where that wuz," Bruce answered as he closed the waffle maker.

"Ok," Tishona said simply as she headed in that direction.

While Tishona separated single slices of cheese off of

a long pre-sliced block and restacked them so that their corners alternated to make them easier to pick up in a hurry Bruce shredded lettuce and added two more waffles to the plate.

"Shoot!" he blurted when they were done. "Got duhstracted. Told Hank I could do Belgian waffles an he'd said 'that'll do' but I coulda swore he said he'd take a few." He then slide two of the waffles off onto other plates and handed one of them to Tishona.

"You lie," Tishona accused with a grin. "You never get distracted in the kitchen."

Bruce shooed her out of the kitchen, "Fetch us some sir'up."

"I can do that," Tishona agreed as Bruce began tearing his waffle into bite sized pieces.

"Smells good," Hank stated as she approached his table. He laid down his newspaper which had a frontpage headline that read: Judge Denies Continuance – Trial to Commence.

"Yeah they do," Tishona admitted. "I'm sorry! I forgot to come pour you some coffee!"

"No worries," Hank dismissed her concern. "Knew where it wuz. Go take care a business. I'm all set."

As Hank was drizzling maple syrup onto his waffle Tishona was heading back into the kitchen with a syrup dispenser. When He finished his waffle he carried his empty plate to a dish cart and sat it in the empty top tub. As he was pouring more coffee for himself the bell over the front door jingled.

***

"When did You get a job here?" Marilyn Roedel asked pointedly when she saw Hank pouring his own coffee.

"This mornin'," Hank replied without hesitating. "Sit yerselfsomewheresan I'll get ta ya in a minute."

"Good morning Ms. Roedel," Tishona said pleasantly as she came out of the kitchen. "I'll be right with you."

When Hank glanced over and saw the scowl on Marilyn's face he shook his head. "Nah, she's sittin' in My section this mornin'," he told Tishona with a wink. "Go on with yerprep work an I'll let ya know if ya get any customers in yer section."

Tishona fought back a grin, nodded her head, and quietly replied, "Yes Sir."

To Marilyn's chagrin Hank snatched up a menu, stuck it under his arm, and then fixed a glass of ice water to take to her. "Lemme know when yer ready ta order."

Marilyn huffed indignantly. "What if I'm Already ready to order?"

"Then order!" Hank snapped back at her. "You want somethin' buhsides water?"

"I, I want sweet tea!" Marilyn blurted after a brief hesitation.

"I'll fetch itferya," Hank told her when she picked up the menu he'd taken to her. When he returned with her tea he had an order pad and pen. "Know whutyerwantin'?"

"Well I'm not sure just yet!" Marilyn blurted when her indecision got the better of her.

"Person'lly, I suggest a Belgian waffle," Hank recommended seriously. "Bet that'd do the trick ferya."

"Fine, but I want Light toast to go with it," Marilyn conceded a moment later.

"Whut'd'ya want with yer toast?" Hank asked as he wrote down her order.

"Butter is fine," Marilyn replied in a softer tone.

"Anythin' else?" Hank asked as he took the menu.

"I don't think so," Marilyn answered quietly.

"Jus' lemme know if ya change yer mind," Hank

stated coolly before turning and ambling over to the order window. "Order in!" he declared as he put the ticket on the order wheel. As he turned the wheel the bell over the door jingled again.

Hank turned to find Rick grinning ear to ear as he walked through the door. "Ya takin' orders?"

"Yep!" Hank answered briskly. "Whut'd'ya want?"

"Coffee fer starters," Rick told him without looking away.

"Sit yerself then," Hank instructed as he picked up the pot of freshly brewed coffee.

Rick glanced over at the table where Hank's newspaper was lying folded up. "Sure is gonna be a perty day."

"Looks it," Hank agreed as Rick turned his cup over. "Know whutyawanna order er do ya need a menu?"

"I ain't in no hurry," Rick confessed with a shrug. "Want the coffee more'nanythin' else."

"The Belgian waffles are a good choice this mornin' if yaain't too picky," Hank offered as he filled Rick's coffee cup.

Rick gave Hank a questioning look which was met with a sly grin and a brief glance towards Marilyn who was preoccupied with a hangnail. "Is that right?"

"Yup, Bruce's havin' a rough start tuhday," Hank informed him in a whisper.

"Waffles sound good as anythin'," Rick decided with a shrug. "I'd take a couple'v'em."

"Anythin' else?" Hank asked, noting Rick's order on the order pad.

"Can I read yer paper?" Rick asked with a smile.

"Don't go messin' it all up," Hank warned.

"Order up!" Bruce shouted from the order window.

"Double that order!" Hank hollered back as he headed towards the window. "Single serve 'em fer

Rick."

"Got it!" Bruce shouted back with a laugh in his voice.

"Here ya go Ma'am," Hank said politely as he placed Marilyn's plate on her table. "Let me know if ya need anythin' else," he instructed as he put a saucer with her light toast next to her plate.

"Thank you," she replied more politely than usual.

"Welcome," Hank said with a nod. "Enjoy 'em."

Marily nodded slightly in return. "I'm sure I will."

"Lookin' like he's fin'llygonna face the music," Rick said, laying the paper down as Hank brought him a plate with two large Belgian waffles on it.

"Looks like it," Hank agreed with a nod.

***

Hank made his way to his favorite table and sat down facing the door. He glanced across the nearly empty café and gave the young waitress, Tishona a slight nod when she glanced at him.

He knew she'd be with him as soon as she finished turning in the order she was taking so he turned over his coffee cup, sat it on its saucer, and slid it to the side of the table.

He opened up his newspaper and scanned the front page. A few minutes later he laid his paper down when he saw her approaching his table with a pot of hot coffee. "G' Mornin' Tish."

"Good morning Sir," Tishona greeted politely.

Hank shook his head and laughed at the young lady's insistence on calling him Sir. "Ya know, even my pappy didn't go by Sir," Hank told her with a grin. "He'd tell folks, 'Don't go callin' Me Sir! I worked fer a livin' in the Navy!' an he shore 'nuff did."

"Do you expect Mr. Miller to be joining you this morning?" Tishona asked as she glanced at the headline on Hank's paper which read: Jury Selection to Commence.

"I reckon he'll be along sooner than later," Hank replied with a soft chuckle.

Tishona glanced about briefly before quietly stating, "I heard he was summoned to report for jury selection."

"Shore 'nuff," Hank acknowledge with a nod. "Course Ole Rick'll slip up an say somethin' that city slicker lawyer of Ole Chester's won't like and he'll kick 'im loose fer sure."

"So you don't think there's any chance he'll serve on the jury?" Tishona asked seriously.

Hank chuckled even louder, "Not a snowball's chance in Hell-O young lady!" he changed what he was saying when he noticed eight year old Katrina watching him.

"Hello," Katrina replied with a twinkle in her eyes.

"How's 'bout ya pay attention tayer breakfast 'stead of whut he's talkin' 'bout," her mother suggested with a yawn.

Katrina giggled softly while stabbing a bite of pancake. "I can't help it if he talks loud," she all but whispered with a grin.

"Not tha point anya know it," her father stated while gesturing towards her plate.

Katrina rolled her eyes as she stuffed the bite into her mouth.

"Are you planning to order or will you be waiting on Mr. Miller this morning?" Tishona asked sweetly as if there had been no interruption.

"Reckon I mise well go ahead an order," Hank told her with a shrug. "No tellin' when they'll get 'round ta questionin' 'im."

"Do you know what you want or would you like a few minutes?" Tishona asked as the bell above the door jingled. "Good morning! Have a seat and I'll be right with you!"

"Well, that young lady made me hungry fer pancakes" he stated while gesturing towards Katrina, "so bring me a short-stack, with a couple'v over-easy eggs an sausage links."

"Anything else?" Tishona asked when Hank glanced at Katrina's father who was taking a bite of bacon.

"Yeah, reckon I could do with a side of extra crispy bacon too," Hank answered decidedly.

"Will do," Tishona said politely. "Do you folks need anything else?" she asked Katrina's parents.

"All good here," her father answered while shaking his head.

"Unless you wanna babysit this comin' Friday night," Katrina's mother suggested with a grin.

"Oh that's above my paygrade I'm afraid!" Tishona replied with a laugh.

Hank had finished his breakfast and sat sipping his coffee while reading his paper when Rick came strolling into the café wearing a dress shirt and slacks instead of his usual T-shirt and blue jeans.

"There's a sight ya won't see ev'ry day," Hank stated with a grin.

"Buhlieve that," Rick replied with a laugh. "These're only ferweddin's, fune'rals, an court."

"Know that's right," Hank agreed after a sip of coffee. "Got some I only wear fer the same things, 'ceptfer my own fune'ral. Got it in my will not ta bury me in those dern things. I wanna be able ta relax."

"Sounds like ya gave it a lotta thought," Rick said with a chuckle as he sat down.

"Shoot, I done decided that a long, long time ago!" Hank declared as he sat his cup down. "Got it in there not ta put my shoes on either far as that goes."

"Whut 'bout yer socks?" Rick asked as he turned his coffee cup over and sat it on its saucer.

"Oh I want those on," Hank stated matter-of-factly. "I'on't want my feet gettin' cold."

"Reckon that makes sense," Rick admitted with a shrug.

"So," Hank began with a gleam in his eyes. "Whut'd'ya say that got ya kicked?"

"Didn' say nothin'!" Rick all but growled.

"Uh huh, I'm 'sposed ta buhlieve that?" Hank asked with a smirk.

"It's True!" Rick insisted as Tishona approached their table.

"Why'd he kick ya then?" Hank asked before getting a sip of coffee.

Rick grinned widely. "Fer a look I reckon. Said he didn't like the way I wuzlookin' at his client."

"What did you do?" Tishona asked as she began to fill Rick's cup. "Give him the evil eye?"

Rick chuckled softly, "Nah, I wuzsmilin' at 'im."

"Oh snap!" Tishona blurted with a laugh. "No wonder he dismissed you!"

"Darn shame too!" Rick said with a grin.

"Uh huh, shore is," Hank agreed with a nod.

"Well, since you're here, what can I get you for breakfast?" Tishona asked politely.

"Thinkin' I'm in the mood fer eggs 'n bacon," Rick replied before sipping his coffee.

"Don't think too hard," Hank needled with a laugh.

Rick ignored Hank's jest. "Lemme get some hashbrowns an some toast ta go with 'em."

"No problem," Tishona said with a smile before leaving to turn in his order.

***

Hank sat at his usual table sipping his coffee and

watching the door of the café for Rick. He'd read his paper front to back and worked part of the crossword puzzle before Rickeventually showed up.

When Rick finally sauntered in and looked around he saw that the small café was even busier than usual. He smiled when he saw his favorite waitress, Tishona, was working.

"Where ya been?" Hank asked after Rick had waved at a few people and greeted a few others just inside the door.

"Down'tathe station," Rick answered with a gleam in his eyes. "Stopped off fer some gas."

"Heard the news?" Hank asked, a smile tugging at the corner of his mouth.

"Heard a time'er two," Rick replied with a snicker. "Bunch a the fellas down there wuztalkin' 'bout it."

"That right?" Hank asked with a grin.

Rick nodded as he pulled out a chair to sit down. "Uh huh, that's right."

"Whut'd'ya know?" Hank asked with a raised eyebrow.

"Know more'nwhut's in yer paper fer shore," Rick told him.

Hank looked at Rick across the top of his cup as he sipped his coffee. "Are yagonna spill the beans'rwhut?"

"Wuzenjoyin' knowin' sumthin' ya didn't fer a change," Rick told him with a smirk.

"Enjoy it while ya can," Hank suggested with a snort. "Might be the only time!"

"G'Mornin Tish!" Rick greeted her as she approached with a pot of coffee.

"Good morning Sir," Tishona replied sweetly. She giggled softly at the delight in their eyes. "Ready to order something to go with your coffee?"

"Oh, I could eat," Rick told her with a wink. "Did ya

eat yet?"

"Nope, weren't all that hungry yet so I wuz a waitin' ferya," Hank answered.

"That bein' the case I'm buyin'," Rick announced.

"Ibuhlieve Ijus' got hungrier!" Hank professed with a chuckle.

"Do you know what you want?" Tishona asked when Rick didn't flinch at the comment.

Hank looked to Rick for a moment. "Hit me with a order a biscuits 'n gravy, hashbrowns, two eggs over easy, a couple a sausage links, an a side a whut he calls burnt bacon."

Rick nodded his approval, "Double it, scramble my eggs, an make mine with a side a whut he calls raw bacon."

"Coming right up," Tishona told them with a smile. "Your order should be out soon," she informed a small family at another table as she went past.

"So, Ole Ron whut were on the jury wuz down at the station," Rick discreetly announced with a grin.

"Oh? Which Ron?" Hank asked with a raised eyebrow.

"Ole Ron Delemore," Rick answered matter-of-factly. "Ain't no way they'd a let Ron Sotomayor be no juror on that case."

"Reckon that's true 'nough," Hank replied with a shrug.

"So Ole Ron says that jus'buhfore Ole Chester's city lawyer wuz 'bout ta give his closin', there wuz a ruckus outside a the courtroom," Rick went on with a smile.

"Whut kind a ruckus?" Hank questioned before getting a sip of his coffee.

"The loud kind," Rick answered with a chuckle. "Said he heard Ole Boon a tryin' ta tell someone they weren't a comin' in. Then a minute later Ole Boon opened that door jus' as wide as he could fer Ole Widow Wilson."

Hank grabbed a napkin to wipe up the coffee he spilled when he laughed into his cup.

"Ole Ron said Widow Wilson eyed Ole Boon as she hobbledinta the courtroom with her walker, an says 'Thaswhut I thought!' as she passed 'im by."

"Hard ta buhlieve Ole Boon even tried ta stop 'er in the first place," Hank said with a smirk.

"Know I woodn't a tried!" Rick admitted while shaking his head. "Ole Ron said Widow Wilson, in her best nightgown, an with curlers in her hair, wuzmakin' her way ta'words the judge when Ole Judge Booker asks, 'Whut's this all about?' an she tells 'im, 'Got it all on tape! Er, got it all on this... this Doohickey!' an held up one a them lil square mem'rydoodads," Rick told Hank in a rush.

"That right?" Hank asked with a smile.

"Yup! Ole Judge Booker goes, 'Whaddya got on there?' Widow Wilson tells 'im, 'Got whut he did ta the skinny brown haired boy whutbrung the papers on it! Got it All!' Ole Judge Booker asks, 'Why'd ya wait 'til now ta bring it in?' an Widow Wilson says, 'Never thought ta look! Only looked a bit ago 'cause someone knocked over my trash an scattered it... turned out ruhcoons done it, But! I Saw whut he did! All on here!" Rick said in practically one breath.

"So that did 'im in huh?" Hank asked with a snicker.

"Yup! Judge Booker called it recess ta review the mem'ry thingamajig even though Ole Chester's city slicker lawyer wuz a throwin' up a fuss sayin' it weren't admissible. 'Course Ole Ron said Ole Judge Booker told 'im he'd danged well be the one ta decide whut were admissible er not in HIS courtroom."

"Bet he did!" Hank blurted with a laugh.

"Ole Ron says they weren't no more'n in Ole Judge Booker's chambers when they heard a bunch a squabblin' an then Ole Judge Booker yelled 'Contempt of Court!' an it got REAL quiet," Rick stated with a snicker.

Hank snorted at the thought but didn't comment. He simply took another sip of his coffee and waited for Rick to continue.

"So, 'course Ole Judge Booker da'clared it admissible, an soon they were showin' it ta the jury. Whelp, shore 'nough Ole Chester could be seen plain as day doin' whut he'd been accused a doin'!" Rick erupted with a gleam in his eyes.
"Ole Ron said Ole Chester sat a hidin' his face in his hands when they were a reviewin' it. Said he were whimpering when they were sent ta deliberate," Rick told him with a snicker.

"Not too surprisin'," Hank pointed out as he set his coffee down.

"Yep! 'Course it wuz the fastest guilty verdict in these parts in years," Rick announced before getting a sip of coffee.

Hank smiled broadly as Rick finally took a slow sip of his coffee. "I don't reckon Ole Judge Booker let 'im off with a light sentence either."

"'Course not! Ole Judge Booker threw the book at 'im. Gave 'im a full twenty five years ferwhut he did."

"That'll learn 'im good!" Hank blurted with a chortle.

"Uh huh," Rick snickered as he put down his coffee cup. "Ole Ron said when Judge Booker handed down his sentence Ole Chester screamed like a lil' girl and then started ta cry like a baby."

"Oh he did?" Hank asked with a chuckle.

"Yep, he were a cryin' and sayin' how it jus' weren't fair," Rick announced with a nod. "Then he made a desp'rate attempt ta run outta the courtroom but Ole Boon reached out an grabbed 'im by the collar as he tried ta run past."

Just as Tishona was setting Rick's food in front of him the bell over the door jingled when a white haired old man in a wheelchair pushed his way inside. Tishona stopped short of her usual greeting when she saw who it was.

He waved at Tishona when she glanced towards him and then pointed at an empty table near Hank and Rick. She smiled in return, and slid one of the chairs out of his way, before heading after a pot of coffee so that she could fill his cup.

"You boys been stayin' outta trouble?" he asked as he rolled up to the table next to them.

Rick just shrugged since his mouth was full.

"Mostly," Hank answered before sipping his coffee. "How you doin' Brent?"

"Got a feelin' that jus' means yaain't been caught," Brent stated with a laugh. "Me? I've been on a roll."
'Knew that wuscomin' buhfore I ever asked,' Hank thought before getting another sip. "Heard the news?"

"The news 'bout Ole Chester?" Brent asked while waving at someone across the diner. "Heard he wus a bawlin' like a baby's whut I heard," Brent said with a chuckle.

"Mhm, that's whut I heard too," Rick commented between bites.

"Twenty five years," Hank said with a gleam in his eyes.

"Yep, don't reckon he'll be catchin' fireflies in a jar any time soon," Brent stated evenly.

TIME TO TELL THE TRUTH
Sonny Collins

When a man turns 65 he realizes that his remaining days are numbered and it might be time to re-evaluate his life. So, here is my story. All the dirty little secrets that I have kept from others through the years are about to be made public. I just hope the world is ready!

I had a normal childhood, with loving parents and two brothers. It wasn't until I reached high school that I became the great lover that has cursed my life through the years. There were too many to name.

Upon graduation my family moved to Kansas, leaving me in Oklahoma. This is when my adventures really began. I was recruited into a secret organization that was so secret I still don't know its name. My recruiter was an army colonel named Big Jake McCord (not sure how he got the name as he was only about five feet tall) who taught me how to defend myself by learning a complex mix of karate, judo, kung fu, and tofu. I also became quite good with a revolver, rifle, machine gun, rocket launcher, and how to push the red button on an atomic bomb (this was always handy in later years for when I went to the casino).

My first mission had me working alone. My cover was as a grocery store cashier. It took me four days to infiltrate the produce scam of the century. Farmers were bringing their goods to us through a backdoor and skipping the middle man to make more money. I stopped that practice cold! Now everything goes through several people before it gets to your table. This keeps the cost up and more profit can be made by the big boys at the top. You have me to thank for this.

My next mission was much bigger. It was 1978 when I was sent to Guyana to help Jim Jones show off his new community called Jonestown. Our government was planning to use this as a base for going into business with the drug lords. While Mr. Jones and I were talking one day about some of his enemies, I made the suggestion he invite them over and poison their lemonade (little did I know he'd use my idea later to commit mass suicide).

It was now the 1980's and I was ready for a more exciting mission. Big Jake sent me to Grenada as an undercover agent. My first kill was made on this trip. I was holding a gun to the head of the communist leader when it accidentally went off (this was easily covered up by sitting him with the rest of his staff before they were executed by machine gun). After I helped Hudson Austin take over the country I realized he was no better than his predecessor, so I contacted Big Jake. He told me to get out of there because President Reagan was going to invade the place.

A few months later I was flown to the White House for a meeting with the President. After he thanked me for all I'd done he gave me my most precious gift - the secret Medal of Honor (not a lot of those are given out). It was to be the first of many I would receive from my dear friend, Ronnie.

In 1986 while on a mission in Libya I phoned the President and said, "Gaddafi and these people are nuts!"

His response was as expected. "Get out of there!"

The next day he bombed Libya.

I moved on to missions in Iraq and Iran. After meeting with Ayatollah Khomeini and finding him to be a really nice guy, I informed the President to side with Iran. Then I tried to broker a deal between the Ayatollah and Saddam Hussein and the Iraqis, but the only thing they had in common was a mutual hate for the United States. But Iraq had no problem taking our money for support.

Luckily I made a deal with the Taliban and we were able to keep Russia out of our business. As Ronnie told me, "It's all about the oil. Keep it coming!"

I then came up with a plan to fund our endeavors to take over the drug trade in Nicaragua by secretly selling weapons to Iran. It was working beautifully until Oliver North got caught shredding top secret papers. Luckily, the scandal never involved my name. I was always able to stay one step ahead of the CIA.

I was aware that the President was given credit for these incidents, but the truth was, they really should have been attributed to me. Some of my finest moments. (And another secret Medal of Honor).

My next mission was to Russia where I told Mikhail Gorbachev to tear down the Berlin wall. Knowing who I was he complied immediately, but somehow Ronnie got the credit once again (yet another secret Medal of Honor for me).

When the President left office I had a tough decision to make - should I stay with the secret organization or retire? After all, I was now 30. Something told me to move to Kansas because that was where all the action was. One of the few times I was wrong.

My new cover was as a KFC restaurant manager (which I held for 31 years). I would now only work for the organization as a free-lance employee (taking only the jobs I wanted). It went unnoticed that I usually took six to eight weeks of vacation a year.

The secret missions had taken a toll on my mental state of being and I found myself needing an outlet. Turned out traveling to the remote desert canyons of the Four Corners region was cathartic for me. I became a serial killer. It started off by accident. I saw this guy backpacking in Utah and stopped to converse with him as we stood on the edge of a steep cliff. The urge to shove him just came over me. His scream echoed across the vast, empty desert and I was hooked. The feeling of exhalation was addicting. Over the next several years I racked up 57 kills. They always looked like accidents and I had no motive. (It was just fun, like tipping cows).

Then I found God. Hard as it was, the killings had to stop. I was like an addict and forced myself into total seclusion for weeks to repress my violent nature. Now I really felt guilty. Killing all those innocent people when I could have been doing some good by getting rid of all the bad people. I let the organization know I was ready to become an assassin.

Obviously, I can't name names, but let's just say a lot of evil drug lords and sex traffickers are no longer on the streets. But after a few years of this I got bored. There had to be something more meaningful than killing people.

I found God again. And he gave me the luck of my life. I became a professional gambler, hitting all the big and small casino's. Fortunes were made and lost in a single day, day after day. The monotony of it drove me to drink. Jamaican rum was my favorite. I became famous as a party hopper. Everyone knew me when I walked into a club. Women threw themselves at my feet. It was the best time of my life. Then I met HER. Jane Seymour was the most beautiful woman I ever met. We danced all night, made passionate love all day. My only mistake was advising her to star in a new television series. Dr. Quinn, Medicine Woman was the ruin of our affair. She went back to Hollywood and I stayed in Kansas with a broken heart that no doctor could mend. Maybe I'll find her again, somewhere in time...

I did find God once again. This time I committed my

energy into building the biggest mega church in the world. Of course the pastor didn't always agree with my ways of getting attention for our cause. I told him if we picketed gay weddings and funerals it could put us in the news. And it did, just not always in a good way.

My fall from grace came when I took a trip to Vegas and met another movie star. Julia Roberts was the most beautiful woman I ever met. We danced all night, made passionate love all day. But I never could get her to come to my best friend's wedding. We parted ways with the knowledge that in our hearts, we would always be together.

The secret organization then came a calling. Big Jake wanted me back to tie up some loose ends for President Bush Junior. I went to Iraq and started the trouble that would finally topple Saddam Hussein. It was a messy job, but someone had to do it. Funny, though, I never did find those weapons of mass destruction.

For the next several years I headed many covert operations, usually pitting one country against another before the United States stepped in to solve the problem.

I was now over 40 and really wanting to retire. So I went to Hollywood and met, yet another movie star. The age difference didn't bother me a bit (she was born the same year as my mother). Ann-Margret was the most beautiful woman I'd ever met. We danced all night, made passionate love all day. We could have been happy together, but she had too much carnal knowledge. I returned to Kansas, the better for having known such a woman.

God again found me. I decided to become a writer of songs and fiction. I took over a Mennonite press and wrote such classics as "The Zombie Bats", "The Flower Girl" and "When Mountains Fell and Geysers Flew." It was a fulfilling life and I was finally content.

Then the Devil came calling. Donald Trump found me through the secret organization and made contact. He really needed my advice after he'd become President. I went to the White House and told him it would make a great Bed and Breakfast, but he needed my advise on more pressing matters. He wanted to know how to connect with the people.

I told him to keep doing what he'd always done. Be a reality star who always stirs up trouble. My best advice to him was to never tell the truth, keep people guessing. And because of me he has become the man he is today.

When I went back to Kansas the Covid bug hit, causing the KFC I'd worked at for 31 years to close. I rang up Dr. Fauci and said that he needed to get this flu under control. Since there was a Pfizer plant in my town I suggested getting them to do something. He got right on it and soon we had a cure thanks to me.

Now with no job I decided to roam the country and follow a pop star. The age difference meant nothing to me (I was old enough to be her dad). Taylor Swift was the most beautiful woman I'd ever met. We danced all night, made passionate love all day. I was the inspiration for her albums "Folklore" and "Nevermore." I didn't mind being a sugar daddy, but when she met some football player I knew it was over between us. Yet, I think she'll regret what could have been.

NASA then needed me. I was secretly sent up to the Space Station several times to solve problems between our astronauts and the commie scum sent up by Russia and China (you might say they are now lost in space).

Upon my return to Kansas I once again found God. Maybe this time it will stick. My next adventure will have me heading to Canada (I know they've been hiding Bigfoot from us).

Now the world has my story and can do with it what it will. And as any 'Trumper' will tell you. This was the absolute, complete truth.

CATCHING LIGHTNING BUGS IN A JAR
Sonny Collins

When I was but a small child
I can remember my grandparents backyard
A warm Oklahoma evening
With the tree frogs singing -
And then I would see them
Like magic they appeared
Flittering through the trees
Toward the rose bushes -
My grandmother would say
"Be gentle with them
They are delicate creatures
Not to be hurt" -
My grandfather would hand me
A clear glass mason jar
With holes punched in the lid
From his screwdriver -
My little hands carefully reached out
Until I caught my prey
A tiny flying insect
Who's tail lit up -
Placing it in the jar
I'd then search for more
Running through the night
Filled with joy -
Soon I'd have so many
That my jar became a lamp
Until it was time to let them go
Back into my dreams.

FIREFLIES
Sonny Collins

How long have I loved you
It's a question hard to answer
Because it is forever

We have climbed mountains together
Walked side by side
Almost as one

Like fireflies dancing through the forest
You light up the path
To my heart

LIGHTNING BUGS AND LICORICE
Sonny Collins

To be a child again
With no worries or cares
Excited for the summer
With its carnivals and fairs

Playing with your friends
Running through the neighborhood
Thinking it would never end
Yet, knowing that it would

After a game of tag
You'd climb into a tree
Dreaming on drifting clouds
Feeling ever so free

Making paper boats
To float along the drain
That flowed down the street
After a cool summer rain

Camping in the backyard
Telling a scary story
Eating licorice
As lightning bugs lit up in glory

Those days are now long gone
But in our memory they stay
Longing for a time
To be a kid at play.

LIGHTNIN' BUG
Sonny Collins

I seem to recall the first time I ever saw a lightning' bug
Was when I ventured over North Carolina way
I was ridin' in a stage with some wealthy folks
As best I recall they was from the big city,
We had stopped for a breather in the piney woods
(I actually had to go take a piss)
Figurin' it was getting dark I didn't go far into the trees
When I saw these here fairy lookin' critters,
They were tiny little creatures flyin' this way and that
I skidaddled back to that stage in a hurry
The passengers must have seen my look of fear
'cause one asked what was the matter?
I weren't sure how to answer that question
Then it happened right then and there
Them strange flyin' insects circled the stage
Causing all sorts of mischief,
One lady said they were beautiful
While her husband scoffed with a snide grin
"They are just another fly to spook the horses"
(Though the horses didn't seem to mind)
When I saw that no one was scared
I took more interest in them lightning' bugs
And that's when I realized they had to be from Mexico
'cause I saw them poop fire.

LOOKING FORWARD
Starla Criser

I can't believe how fast the years are flying by. How is it I'm 73 already? 73? It just doesn't feel possible I'm that old. Not that I will EVER consider myself "old."

Time and memories get so mixed up in my mind. The years and experiences blur together. Wasn't it just yesterday my dad created this odd-looking way for me to learn to ride a bicycle? He took a perfectly good child's bicycle and added training wheels made of the backend of a large tricycle. Even at seven, I felt embarrassed by the contraption. But it kept me safe. No way could I fall over.

A decade later, my dad was still up to creative nonsense. My folks let me have parties a lot and they were always fun. My friends knowing my dad would always have some new thing to try out. At this particular party, he came up with this game attachment that we tied around our waists. Attached to a belt was a ping-pong paddle with a ping-pong ball tied to it. You had to wiggle and wriggle and contort your body to hit the ball. We laughed until we collapsed at each other's bizarre attempts.

Along came my driving years and my first car: the ugliest green Studebaker you've ever seen. Built as tough as a tank with a ton of quirks. The front seat wouldn't stay up. So, my trusty dad solved that problem by bracing it up with a board from the backseat. But he couldn't solve the annoying problem it had by flinging open the passenger door on right turns. Somewhere along the time I had it, the door-flinging issue stopped. Who knew why? The car had its heyday, though, when it was the decorated car at Steve and my wedding.

Life moved along all too quick after those early

years. I got married and have stayed married now for fifty-three years.

I had a child that I just knew would be a boy—except I was wrong. Not the first time I've been wrong in my life. Yet that child has turned into the most amazing woman, and I couldn't be prouder. How she survived having me as a mother is beyond my understanding. I mean, I had no idea "how" to be a good mother, how to teach her all the right things about being a good and caring person, how to become a strong, independent woman that could also find a wonderful man and have a good marriage herself. I just got lucky.

During my seven decades—how weird is it to say that? Anyway, in all that time, I've lived my life fully and happily. I don't see things as black or white, but as many shades of colors. I see possibilities, not impossibilities. I make quick decisions, sometimes wishing I had taken a bit more time to think things through. I will try almost anything within my physical abilities and, so far, have regretted nothing I've attempted.

At this point in my life, I have several less-than-wonderful physical issues: diabetes, hypertension, neuropathy, and not the best eyesight. What I also have is endless determination. I want to continue doing as much and as many things as I can. I want to keep trying, to keep believing, to keep caring, and to keep helping others.

I look forward to another twenty or more exciting and challenging years.

NOT A BAD VACATION, BUT...
Starla Criser

The trip from the Highlands had started so well,
Yet driving along, we suddenly thought, "What the hell?"

Our plan had to been to look for Nessie on Loch Ness.
We couldn't travel on without fixing our error, that mess.

Retracing our route would cost us time and daylight.
But we had to do it, not give up our plan without a fight.

Back we went, watching for the loch eagerly this time.
We left our car and walked along the bank, pleased with no climb.

Squinting, we searched and searched for any sign of her.
Nada, nothing. Not even a faint stirring of the water.

We finally gave up and went on our way.
Maybe next time she would come out and play.

WHERE, OH WHERE?
Starla Criser

The enormous world map is spread across my mattress.
I've been thinking and thinking about where to go.
My mind is awhirl with too many places, such distress.

My stomach growls and I reach for a slice of pizza.
How do I decide with so many possible places?
I glance at Italy, pondering maybe the leaning tower of Piza.

I scrunch my nose as I taste something strange: mustard.
What's that doing on my meat and veggie pizza?
Never mind that, I must decide on my trip, but this is hard.

Should I go by ship, or by car, or rent a motor-home to go far?
I need to narrow this down to the United States or abroad.
But I want to go everywhere, maybe ride a train with a domed car.

I get up to find my laptop and the useful mouse.
I'm better on the computer than with a fold-out map.
Wandering around, I feel comfy here in my beloved house.

Maybe I'll just stay home.
No, no... I'm restless and ready to roam.

ONE LAST TIME
Jana Dahmen

A Chapter from the Cameo Trail Series

~Willheim Brandt

It's the destiny of every West Texas cowboy to take one last ride home and for Tavy Brandt, this final trip came much too early for such a good man. At least sunshine had chased away the harsh elements of the most recent storm blown in from the north. The crispy, breezy air was a reminder of winter's stubborn hold over the weather. Cold, wind, and precipitation would remain a hurdle until the time came to plant seeds in the fields again.

The Brandts knew of lonesome trails leading away from Albuquerque in South Texas to their home place near Sweetwater in West Texas. They'd meander like the crows fly to shave miles off of the trip. Morgan scouted ahead picking the best route for Mateas to maneuver the wagon carrying Tavy's body home. Katrina, his sister, followed the wagon. Side-by-side Will and his new bride brought up the rear.

Will felt a profound responsibility for the girl Tavias so loved and wanted to protect. Her face showed no signs of emotion, neither of sorrow nor of peace. She voiced nary a complaint or made any request. Will watched over her with the eyes of his heart and wondered how she was really faring during this difficult situation she had no control over.

Tavy and she were all set to marry before he'd been murdered. In facing his death, her silence was deafening to Willheim. He was quite uneasy without having a clue how Valentine felt about being forced to marry him instead of her first choice. He could not read her mind and only guessed at ways to help her along. Anguish filled his thoughts with many unasked questions.

She wasn't toughened to the rigors of riding a horse such a long distance or being exposed to the constant cold. He worried she'd most likely be saddle-sore before they made it home. He was concerned the length of this trip would physically weaken her. It was daunting to have the welfare of another human, who was so small and underfed, in his care. He didn't bear the weight of his charge lightly.

On the back of the gray mare he'd given her this morning, she appeared passive and fragile like he imagined an angel might look. Tavias had picked a beautiful woman, and this was his rightful love story. Will felt like a trespasser. He'd inherited his brother's shy beauty for better or worse, forever and ever. It seemed impossible Val was his wife, and he was her husband. He vowed to do right by the gift Tavias had handed him.

Mrs. Willheim Brandt, what a treasure to receive! My brother, you were cheated, but I promise to love and care for your dream carefully.

Tavias was the one who had set this scenario into motion. Under attack and against all odds, he'd hurriedly scratched a note. Then, he had passed it off to Winston, a boy who could neither read nor write. The fact the message even reached Will was a true miracle!

The memory of Tavy sacrificing his dying breath to petition Will to save his Valentine was haunting. At the time, Will had no idea what he was promising his older brother, but it wouldn't have made any difference. He'd have done anything for him, anything!

The caravan escorting Tavy homeward had not been moving any faster than Mateas could respectfully drive the wagon carrying his coffin. All the while Mateas sang low, sad songs in his rich voice lending to the backdrop of mourning. An hour before sunset, Morgan chose the sight of their first camp. They took care of the horses and laid a fire to provide light, warmth, hot food, and to keep critters at bay during the night.

Kat encouraged Valentine with short observations and one-sided chatter. The two walked off together to take care of their personal business away from the men. Will's eyes followed them until they were out of sight. The compassion he held for Val in her grief and uncertainty was strong.

The men cooked a generous hot supper of side meat, fried potatoes, and biscuits cooked done in a covered, iron skillet. The meal was followed with a tasty treat of canned peaches. They sat together afterwards and sipped black coffee together until the large granite pot was emptied. The fire was fortified from larger pieces of wood they'd gathered and banked to last well into the night. Bedrolls had been spread out before sunset around its heat. A saddle was placed at the end of each to serve as a head rest.

Before calling it a night, Morgan said, "We'll head out in the morning after breakfast. Pa has our telegram by now, and he'll be watching the road anxiously for us to ride in with Tavy."

Mateas closed with a few words from the Bible and assured Valentine again how glad they were to have her in the family. He offered a prayer, followed by amens from everyone.

Will retrieved the worn quilt Val had wrapped around her this morning. It had been put in the wagon after he purchased the wool coat and other things to keep her warm. He spread the thick coat over her bedroll for added insulation and put the old quilt on top. His own bedroll was near hers.

As soon as the camp settled with only the sounds of sleeping, Will leaned over from his bedding to check on his girl again. He had something he wanted, no, needed to say to her.

"Are you still awake, Valentine?" he whispered.

Seeing her eyes were open, he continued.

"Life altering circumstances have happened to us really fast. We're both the same people we were, but our two paths have joined as one. We're both shaken but will adjust in time to the new order of things if we're patient with each other.

"I can't know what you're thinkin', but I want ya to know I consider us a team working on the same side of the fence. I'll take care of you and make sure you're safe. Take all the time ya need to get comfortable with me.

"Don't be afraid 'cause I won't rush ya or hurt ya. Tavy would tell you the same about me if he could. I expect nothing from you, Girl, but I'll wait until you're ready for me. Do you understand what I'm sayin', Val?

"I swore to Tavy I'd find you and take you with me to his people. Marrying ya was the only way ta keep my promise. We'll go slow and sort the details out as we go. You'll see.

"Don't fret yourself on none of it. We'll find the way to each other. You rest now, we've got hard day in the saddle tomorrow."

Gently, he smoothed the quilt anew and brushed a tear from her wet cheek. Only then did he notice Tavy's gold watch she was holding in her fist. Once again, he saw her clearly through the eyes of his heart. She was suffering the loss of someone she loved the same as he was. Out of empathy, he lightly kissed her forehead. This impulsive gesture surprised him, but it felt right.

Will sat on his bedroll by the fire while he smoked an

Ole Shenandoah Cheroot, the best cigarillo wrapped in brown tobacco leaves a cowboy could buy. He heard Valentine shifting under the weight of the covers.

Sleep tight, my darling girl. We'll build a family of our own and raise horses. Life will be good. I won't let you or Tavy down.

PRYVIT [Hello] 6PAT [Brother]
Jerry J. Fanning

Oh my God. The sob caught in his throat choking him. Gasping for breath he calmed himself.

"Is this a fake," he asked in his Russian language.

The voice on the line speaking fluent Russian replied, "It is not fake."

"Well then I'm in. When Ukraine soldiers come, do I just kneel down or what? Do you promise not to film me while this is happening so you can pass it on to our superiors?"

"You will be given instructions on how to lay down your weapon and turn yourself in. When you get to the front lines call us immediately."

With the enemy spotting so many unwilling participants the Ukraine strategists realized there might be another way to end this extraordinarily bloody war. As the Russian soldier closed his phone, it hit him that more of his exhausted comrades might join him. The note, pressed into his hand as they hunkered down in the muddy ditch to avoid the howitzer shells, had said only one thing with a phone number, "I want to live." He heard the whisper, "Call this, I'll be behind you as soon as I can."

Right there in the freezing ditch he now knew there was a God. And God was real. He'd been praying for days, just little snippets. "Help me, God. I'm so cold, help me". The voice on the line had told him, "Your voice is distorted to shield your identity. Do you understand that? It's a risk but we can help you if you are serious about defecting. We have strict protocols that are clearly put in place in advance to insure your safety. You must wave a white cloth, remove the magazine from your gun, point it at the ground, and remove your helmet and body armor.

"What about my unit, how do I get away?"

"We can coordinate with special units to extract you safely."

By this time he was quietly crying, listening with all his being. Maybe, just maybe he would live and be reunited with his family. An image of his beautiful humble wife and his two little boys just caused him to cry harder. After the call had ended on the flip phone he'd hidden for a long time, he pushed it down to the bottom of an inside pocket of his military coat. He'd need to call the number when he thought he was close to the front and they'd give him further instructions.

He wouldn't let himself believe he wasn't going to die. He couldn't let himself hope that much, not just yet anyway. Once he got to the Ukrainians and in their care, he trusted he'd be treated fairly. After all they were willing to go to great measures to get him out safely. Were they not trying to do good by getting him away from the prison that was the Russian military? His commander didn't care if he died, but strangers, the enemy no less, did. It was ironic. He'd never dreamed he'd be saved by the enemy! But he was so sick of this damned war. He was convinced now that Putin was power hungry and no amount of defeat was going to deter him from deploying another 300,000 troops again and again to prove that he, the supreme power could squash Ukraine and kill as many men as he could to win his objective. You can't win with a leader like that.

Other men in his unit had slowly been disappearing and until the dirty stained note had been pressed into his hand, he thought they were dying. But now he wondered if they had defected like he was planning. If it worked, and he'd done some serious praying, he might live. If the Ukraine's were merciful and followed through, he might be held somewhere that was warm and be given something to eat. He hadn't even considered until now that the reason his stomach hurt so much was that he wasn't just hungry, his bladder and kidneys were protesting from no water for days.

He shook off his day dreaming and reached into his pocket for his white handkerchief. It wasn't very white anymore but it would do. He tied it around his gun barrel and slowly crawled out of the ditch. The firing had momentarily paused so he held his guns high over his head as he could. He was just going to take the chance that it would be seen and he'd make a run for it. Maybe they'd think he was in shell shock and just let him go. He'd keep his helmet on until he was out of sight of his unit. Maybe they wouldn't suspect anything. Even as cold as it was he could feel the sweat under his shirt.

"God up there, I'm talking to you. Can you hear me? Please, please protect me now. You know the ugly Russian commander. Just throw scales over his eyes. I gotta just keep running. Oh, I see the guy behind the cannon. Time for me to shed this helmet and body armor"; he stopped a minute and shed like a snake. His 'white flag' was again flying in the wind over his head.

Tears began rolling down his cheeks making them feel frozen. The Ukrainian guys started cheering. There was absolute purpose in his strides until he reached them. He was safe! A bunch gathered around him and even through the language barrier they were all just guys, slapping him and each other on the backs cementing their friendship and good will. One of them pointed at himself and said "Maxim" so Damien indicated himself and said his name. They repeated his name and took turns shaking his hand, My God, they were brothers in kind just born in different countries.

The taller one took his hand and motioned with his head to go this way. Damien was ready. Stumbling over the rough frozen ground, his stomach growled.

"We've got a few things to talk about, then we'll find you some food and a hot shower." The guy spoke pretty good Ukrainian and Damien knew a few words, but not enough to understand much. But he understood "food and warmth". Tears came again at the mention of those comforts.

No matter what hoops he'd be asked to jump through he knew he was safe now and he'd eventually see his precious family again. The tears just kept coming, noticed now by the Ukraine guy. "Hey man, you're safe with us now; we're friends. We figured that not every Russian wanted to fight us. So now we're not enemies; we're friends". And with that as they reached a building the guy stopped, turned to Damien, and then pulled him in for a bear hug. "Pruvit, 6pat !"

QUANTUM ENTAGLEMENT
Jerry J. Fanning

The intense rain had stopped. Now it was so quiet. She heard the cheep of the baby pheasants calling to their mother hen out in the grassy circle around the house. The sun broke through the pink clouds as she stood staring at them remembering a time 25 years ago. And then there he was all 5 feet 11 and three quarters he insisted he was. Twenty-five years had passed since he'd been gone. Gone not in body but in life. His life had been gone. After you'd been married to him and shared his bed for over twenty-five years, you knew him in and out.

Now he stood there looking exactly the same. His silver-belly Stetson, pearl button snap shirt, Wranglers, and Roper shoes. And, of course, the mustache and crooked grin. None of that mattered now; he was here. She couldn't believe it, her mouth hanging open. Was it really him or a ghost? Her eyes clearly held questions so…he better do some explaining.

"You heard of quantum entanglement, right? I know you wrote a story about us. it goes much further than you can imagine. Your belief that you and I are not separated by time or space is right. It's true. When the time, but not as you know it, of total alignment of certain stars occurs, a shift is manifested in everything you've believed about life and death. It doesn't matter that you thought I died 25 years ago.

I'm here now looking exactly as you remember, right? Damn you look good! Our love didn't go away. It's forever. I'm yours like you are mine forever. I know you've remained faithful to me all these years. I know these things. I'm not God but I <u>am</u> His right-hand man. It's just something written in the stars. But now I'm here and I'm yours."

Unconsciously licking her lips, she had tried to listen patiently. Her eyes were glued to his sensual lips that just kept talking. She just wanted to kiss him and never let go.

"It's been so long!" she moaned.

"Yeah it has. Now…where's your bedroom?"

THE DANCE RECITAL
Mike Freed

My attendance started out somewhat, obligatory,
A grandfather's duty to watch the culmination,
Of days, weeks, months- no years of hard work and practice,
A typical male's reaction I suppose.

But I found myself caught up in it all, the music, and costumes and dancers!
Of course, I liked my granddaughters' performances the best...
But I no longer dreaded the rest!

I became fascinated by it all and began to ponder what might make each
dancer tick? What or who motivated them to perform?
I wondered what lessons and skills many would take from these years,
As it was clear most would not make it their career!

I mused as to why the girls outnumbered guys 30 to 1,
And marveled at the courage of those few brave souls.

And I could not help but laugh at the antics and efforts of the little ones,
And who wouldn't appreciate their carefully choreographed finale,
As each in turn galloped across the stage,
Most pausing briefly to blow kisses, curtsy, and wave!

Oh, that we all could live our lives with the freedom and joy of those tiny
dancers,
And be likewise appreciated for our efforts!

FOUR LESSONS
Mike Freed

#1Live what you believe –"Grandma Elsie's Prayer Book"
With pages worn smooth from the tracing of her hand,
The ink gone,
It didn't matter,
She had all the prayers memorized,
And she lived them day by day!

#2 Always give thanks –"Grateful Knees"
My knees creak and snap and pop and hurt,
and sometimes when I step wrong, they send lightning bolts of pain!
but I rejoice and give God praise for I can walk while many cannot!

#3It is rarely too late to do something positive– "Time to Dance"
It's been a while since I sat down to play with words,
Letting them come to life and leap on to the page,
Rhythmic images, tap dancing as I type.
Inked footprints of imagination, choreographed with emotion and delight.
Do you hear the music? Can you sense the energy and light?
Let's bring joy and brightness into this dark night!
While there's still a chance,
Let's join the dance!

#4 A well lived life includes things done just for fun –"Brewed to Perfection"
I paused to write some poetry in the early morning night,
But the words were slow in coming, the time didn't seem quite right.
So, I put them away for another day and let them percolate,
I had my breakfast and coffee, a better time to await.
The next morning, brewed rhyme poured forth, but its flavor was quite quaint,
Just this little ditty, a profound creation, it positively ain't!

THE WORLD IS A MESS!
Mike Freed

I pray in sighs and moans and groans some days,
over a world in turmoil and assaulted on all sides by the enemy!
I struggle to find words; I struggle to find hope!
As for myself I battle complacency and indifference and feelings of futility,
as I comfortably exist!
I feel powerless to help … though in reality, there is much I can do!
I can offer my prayers in words and in vocalization too deep for words!
I can offer my dollars, as fish and bread with prayers that God will use them
and bless them and multiply them beyond anything we can imagine!
The enemy presses hard all around us and some days even within us,
but the victory is already won in your Son!
He has overcome sin and death and evil and this world for our behalf!
Therefore, in the midst of this mess, we will proclaim His great love and
mercy and compassion and power!
We will call upon Him saying, "Lord, have mercy!" Confident that he has
heard our prayer and is working for good in all of this…
though perhaps often, we cannot see it!

PET SINS
Mike Freed

Pet sins. Seemingly little sins, they are vicious wild animals.
Though we try to tame them, always they are ready to bite and devour!

Pet sins.   Often little sins, with big roots who have grown deep into our
being,
Sometimes they sit dormant, and we think we have weeded them out,
But they lie there waiting for the right time to sprout and regrow.

Pet sins.   A part of us wants them, desires them, needs them.
We have perhaps convinced ourselves that they are not even sins at all.
They have so overpowered and undermined our true self that we often don't
even admit they are there… Yet they are unhealthy and intent on destroying
us.

Forgive us and change us, dear Abba of life, for we feel powerless to change
ourselves!

EMBRACING THE DREAM
Mike Freed

Near dead hands and feet, charred and emerging from a fire!
New hands and feet, a child's hands and feet embrace them, soothe them,
redeem them and bring them new life, urgently, showing them the way out of
the ashes and the flames!

  Then it all fades…
and I am awakened to the reality,
that the urgency may be due more to a near bursting bladder,
than actually connected with the dream.

Extricating myself from the blankets and bedsheets,
I lumber on throbbing knees to the bathroom to relieve myself.
My next thought is to head back to bed,
but the haunting images of that early morning,
cause me to pause,
and to retreat instead to my small office to write,
lest the lingering vision, along with its emerging message be completely lost.

As I put fingers to keyboard, I am hopeful that the dream,
has loitered long enough and well enough to move me, and perhaps others
forward,
with renewed childlike,
hope and trust,
joy and compassion,
peace and love,
and healing!

FOREIGN FOUND HOME
Duane L Herrmann

Sam opened the door to their apartment and stood in shock. What he saw didn't register in his mind. The room was empty, and beyond, the dining room was also empty. There were random bits of trash on the floor, but that was all. Dazed he looked around in disbelief. There in "his" corner was "his" chair, old, worn and comfortable, which his wife had hated. On the seat was a piece of paper which he assumed was trash.

Sam had come home from work after a very stressful day. Everything that could go wrong, did. He just wanted to collapse into bed. Xenia had said they were to go to Nicole's for dinner. Sam didn't want to. He found Nicole to be a nuisance and her husband an obnoxious bore, but Xenia had made the commitment, there was no getting out of it.

He could barely stand in his exhaustion and shock. He dropped his coat and the papers in his hand and staggered over to the chair, collapsing into it. The chair reacted immediately by reclining with the weight of his body. Sam just curled up in oblivion.

Sam woke up and noticed the room was dark except for light coming in through the partially opened front door. Why was it open he wondered. Had he not shut it? He stiffly got up and shut the door. When he returned to the chair, he noticed the piece of paper he had curled up on. Only now, it seemed particularly placed. He turned on the floor lamp by the chair, one he had hated from the moment Xenia had brought it home as, 'a bargain, I just couldn't pass up,' and picked up the piece of paper.

"SAM" was written on the front. He opened the half-folded paper and read:

"Get a life! I've left to do that. Don't follow." Signed,

X.

Sam collapsed back into the chair, stunned, and slept again.

When Sam woke again, it was totally dark outside and he was hungry. He walked stiffly to the kitchen to see if anything was there that could be eaten.

The fridge was nearly empty, but that was no surprise. There was a cold hot dog from last night. He picked up the plate it was on and turned to put it in the microwave. There was no microwave. He sighed, and began to eat it cold. His mouth was dry so he began to look for a glass. Only a few odds and ends were left in the cupboard, he didn't care. The water he drank helped wash down the food. At least it was something.

'Call Ted,' came his next, faint thought. He pulled his phone from his pocket and did just that.

"Hi, guy!" Ted's breezy voice came over the phone as if he hadn't a care in the world and nothing had happened. Sam couldn't respond. He just stared at the wall.

"Sam, Sam? Are you there?"

Sam tried to make words but only sounds came out.

"What's going on, Bud?"

More gurgling sounds came from Sam's throat.

"What the hell is going on?"

"I... Xen...," was all Sam was able to say, then he dropt the phone. "SAM! SAM!!! What the Hell?!?"

Sam couldn't respond.

"Are you home? I'll be right over Bud. Hang in there!" Ted abruptly ended the call.

Sam simply sank to the floor and began to sob.

"SAM!" Ted burst into the place a short time later. "What the HELL?!! Where are...?" Ted strode into the kitchen and stood over Sam. "Can you get up?" He asked in a sympathetic voice.

Sam managed to nod his head a bit and reached out an arm.

"Never mind," Ted said and plopped himself down on the floor next to Sam, then put his arm around Sam's shoulder. "Can you tell me what the hell happened here?"

"She... She..." Sam tried to begin, then sobbed some more.

"Xenia?"

Sam nodded.

"She stripped the place and left?"

Sam nodded again.

"Was there a note?"

Sam pointed to the other room.

"I'll look at it later. Have you eaten? Never mind. You gotta' get outa' here. This would depress anyone." Ted stood up. "Come on."

Sam simply raised his hand a bit.

"Let me help you up," Ted reached down and pulled Sam to his feet. "Got your keys and wallet?"

Sam nodded.

"Alright, lets go." Ted shut and locked the door as he herded Sam out of the apartment and to his own car. "Get in," he held the passenger door open for Sam.

"My God, Sam!" Ted exclaimed as he drove away. "What the hell was going on in her head? I know you don't know. I just find it hard to take. She... She...." Ted hit the steering wheel with his fist. "You don't deserve this! The bitch!"

Sam moaned in despair.

"Alright," Ted said after having driven aimlessly for a while. "How about McCory's?"

Sam simply stared straight ahead.

"You don't care do you?" Ted asked. "McCory's it is."

A few minutes later, Ted parked the car and they sat in silence for a while.

"Can you get yourself out?" Ted finally asked.

Sam nodded and they went into the restaurant.

"Just tea," Ted told the waiter who stood there. "We both need to be able to think." Ted stared at Sam for a while, now seeing him clearly for the first time. "He needs a real meal," pointing to Sam. "Actually, we both do. Two chicken fried steaks with broccoli." He knew what Sam liked, but also knew it didn't matter tonight.

"Sam. You're thirty-six years old; you've been with her for ten years and she's refused to marry you all this time. Now, you know why. This is a good thing, Sam. You can find someone better.

"And," Ted continued, "you've been pushing yourself for how many years in the company? Don't answer that, I know. And, how often have you taken a vacation? I know the answer to that to: Zero. As your friend, AND your boss, I'm ordering you six month's leave, fully paid, beginning immediately. And, paid transportation to..., to anywhere out of the U.S. You need a break, man. And, I'm ordering you to take it." Ted paused and took a breath.

"And, I will repeat this if I have to, you are NOT to come to work tomorrow. That is an order. Do you understand?" Ted peered into Sam's eyes and held them until Sam nodded. "And, probably your place isn't fit to sleep in tonight, so I'm putting you up at a hotel, company expense. You get your ass out of this country A.S.A.P. Is that clear?" Again, Ted stared into Sam's eyes until he nodded agreement.

"Good."

Being away from the ravaged apartment, in a place where people were behaving normally, helped Sam begin to feel more normal and real. The shock of

Xenia's actions began to fade. When the food came, he was surprised to discover that he really WAS hungry and he ate gratefully.

After the relaxing meal, Ted took him to the hotel the company used and secured him a room for a week. He didn't want Sam to feel pressured to do anything for the next few days.

"You can't make good decisions after a shock like that," Ted explained.

Over those next days, Sam learned that Xenia had cleaned out their joint bank account, maxed out their joint credit cards, as well as stripping the apartment of nearly everything except his clothes. She'd left him a pillow and an old blanket on the floor to sleep on. Sam disposed of the rest, only keeping a few things of sentimental value which Ted said he could hold for him, as well as some of his clothes, and gave up the apartment. He didn't want to return there ever again. He also booked a flight to Germany.

Germany was a country Sam had always been interested in. His family was from there, somewhere. He wasn't sure who or when, maybe now was the time to find out. By the end of the week, he was flying over the ocean for the first time for pleasure, not work, no pressure. It was a strange experience not to have to rehearse an agenda for the company, or memorize information about a potential client. He wondered if he was even allowed to fly without any of that. He marveled at how different it was.

In the Frankfort airport, or Flughafen, he went to the train station, the Bahnhof, and bought a ticket from the machine. He didn't care where, so selecting a ticket was easy. He just punched buttons by words he could not read.

When the ticket came out, he looked at it, trying to

decipher what to do next. It said: "Gleis 8." Above the tracks were signs that said, "Gleis 7, Gleis 8, Gleis 9," so he walked to Gleis 8. There was a time stamped on the ticket, or Fahrkarte, "14:24." He figured that meant 2:24 pm. He had only about a half hour to wait.

At the appointed time, a train pulled up. The destination on it was the same as on his Farhkarte, so he got on. Sam had seen a chart on the wall of the station of the stops this train made. He assumed the end city was a rather large one. He didn't want that. He wanted to go to a smaller town, a village, or Dorf. He wanted to experience the "real" Germany, not a commercialized, or touristy version. He had written down the names of some of the towns before the end of the line and decided he would get off at one that looked small enough and "felt" good. He wasn't sure what that meant, exactly, but he was done with the planning in minute detail that Xenia had always insisted on. 'Have a little leeway,' he had said to her until she had erupted over his "irresponsibility" and "lack of attention to details." The idea of being spontaneous was alien to her.

He was going to try it his way this time, just to see what might happen. He had six months, as well as the bonus Ted had given him, and Ted's assurance that the firm's attorney's would do what they could about the maxed out cards. He had said Sam needed some time without worries. He gave him a company card to charge expenses. This would be separate from the joint accounts what would now be tied up. He wasn't to worry about expenses. He'd never had a real vacation in his life, now was the time.

As the train rolled through the countryside, Sam reviewed what he would need in his destination town: a hotel or some type of "Gasthaus," access to a bank to withdraw and convert money, a market to buy groceries, a bakery, because he wanted fresh bread and, at least, one local place to eat. Since he wouldn't know if a town did or did not have those things, it had to look big enough to have those things. If the town was near the end of the line, and the bigger town at the end, he figured he could go to the bigger town occasionally if needed.

The first town on the list of names looked way too small, so small Sam was surprised the train stopped there at all. He could see only six houses. Were the others hidden? The second town looked like a comfortable size, so he got off. Several others got off too. None of them had luggage, so he assumed they lived there. Sam stood on the platform, wondering what to do next..

"Bitte," Sam approached one man walking away. "Who ist Gasthaus?" He asked.

"Wolfersburger? Oder, Neigenswanger?" The man replied.

"Neigenswanger," Sam replied, having no idea what the difference might be.

"Kom," the man said, motioned with his hand, and abruptly began to walk away. Sam didn't know much German, but he had worked on saying that one sentence; the first one is the most important he figured. And, "Kom," with the hand gesture of 'follow me,' was pretty clear, so Sam followed with his bags.

They walked two "blocks," which were not really blocks in any sense that Sam was used to, but there were intersections of winding streets, then the man stopped and pointed down a side street.

"Dort," the man said to Sam as he pointed.
Sam looked down the street and saw a sign hanging out from a building: "Neigenswanger."

"Danke, Danke," Sam thanked the man with a nod

and began to walk in that direction. As he walked, Sam began to rehearse his next first line: Do you have a room with one bed.

He walked up several steps to the door. Inside was the expected counter with an obvious bell to ring to call for attention. Sam rang the bell.

"Grüss Gott," a woman greeted him as she came in from the back.

"Grüss Gott," Sam replied. "Haben, Sie, Zimmer mit einem Bett?" A room with one bed.

"Ja," the woman answered with an affirmative nod. "Wie viele tage?"

Sam knew "tage" meant "day," so he knew she was asking how many days did he want the room.

"Ein Monat," Sam answered quickly. He figured a month was enough time to get his bearings and decide what he would want to do next.

"Ja, ja," the woman agreed, nodding her head.

Sam took out the charge card, he had noted the sticker for it on the door.

"Gut, gut," she said, then asked, "Name und Adresse?"

"Sam Gantz," he answered and she wrote it down with no question. Sam was only slightly surprised; most people asked how to spell his last name. Then he gave her Ted's address, he had none of his own, her head popped up and stared at him as he said, "Kansas, U.S.A."

"Willkommen!" She smiled broadly at him. "Mein Sohn lebt in Chicago. Bist du nach Chicago gegangen?" She bubbled in delight, beaming.

"Ja," Sam answered. He understood that she had said her son lived in Chicago and asked, had Sam been there. "Oft."

"Grosse Stadt," she replied, still beaming and opened

her arms wide to demonstrated the size of the city. "Ich gehe nächstes Jahr," she continued with obvious pride. She was going next year.

"Gut, gut," Sam said automatically, and smiled and nodded in return.

"Enjoy, room," she said slowly and deliberately as she gave Sam a key and pointed up the stairway.

"Danke," Sam replied. As he picked up his bags to go up to the room, he heard her go to the back room giggling, then burst into a torrent of German which Sam couldn't follow. He didn't even try.

Sam easily found the room and entered it. He saw that it was plain, simple, basic: just perfect. Xenia would have hated it and refused to stay. Sam thought it was wonderful. There was no separate bathroom, that was at the end of the hall. He didn't mind. This wasn't a large Gasthaus, there couldn't be more than a dozen rooms on this floor, if that many.

He put his suitcase down on the chair against the wall, then stretched out on the bed. As he enjoyed the possibility of stretching, he began to realize that no one he knew would know where he was. It was the first time in his life that his location was unknown. No one could intrude on him. No one could demand that he come and do something. Oh, people could call him, if he was in an area of service, but he was so far away, he could not drop everything and run to respond. For the first time in his life, his time was his own with no responsibilities to anyone! How unreal!!!

His mother had seen him primarily as a labor force. Every day, as soon as he walked in the door from school, she had a list of jobs for him to do. No time to do homework, if he had any – he had to do her work. IF there was time left over from that, then she would demand that he quickly do his homework before he went to bed. No one lived near around them, the next closest house was over a mile away, so he had no place to escape to. Weekends were worse than school days. Both days, all day, of weekends, were filled with work. At least on school days, he had most of the day away from home. At school he could relax somewhat. At least none of the teachers yelled at him. They mostly left him alone. He was a quiet student, did his work and his grades were satisfactory. They all felt he could do better, but in the brief times they had seen his mother, they knew he needed no more pressure from them. The other students were a different story.

To them, he was weird. Weird was bad. Weird had to be taken down, so they were always on him. Not long after every school year had started, he would find a way to stay in the classroom after the others had left. The different teachers found ways for him to stay busy, even if just to read a book. Reading was good.

Now, he was away from everyone who knew him. This was freedom he had never known before. It was amazing. He slept a deep, exhausted sleep.

His first act, when he woke up, was to take a shower. It was late afternoon, plenty of time before supper, or Brotzeit – bread time, the evening meal of coldcuts and breads, many kinds of bread. He had slept better than usual on the plane, but the nap was wonderful! He didn't realize how much relaxing he needed to do. This was not a business trip, he didn't have to push himself. How strange.

After his shower, clean, relaxed, refreshed, Sam looked out the window, across the town and between the red roofs. In the distance, he could see wooded hills. They didn't look too far away, just a couple of miles. Maybe he could hike there, he wondered. That would be interesting. There are no forests or hills like that in

Kansas.

As he left the Gasthaus, Sam could smell cooking aromas in the air, not like home when exhaust was the only thing in the air. After walking a bit, and keeping track of his directions because there were no square blocks, he came to a place to eat. He ordered something with "brat" in the name, and felt confident it would be good. It was.

The next few days, Sam spent simply walking around the little town. He found a Bank, a Bäckerei and a Markt, just as he needed. He also found the little Friedhof with all the graves decorated as individual flower gardens. A few people where there tending the grave gardens, there was even a water spigot in the center for watering the flowers.

"I'm not in Kansas anymore," Sam mused as he watched them for a while, then walked on. It never occurred to him to walk through the gate and get a closer look at the graves. Why should he?

In the center of the village was the church, a very old stone building. A large stone, at the bottom of the door, beside it, had the date of 1647 carved into it. He was sure the date was a significant one in the life of the building. He cautiously pulled the door, and it opened. Slightly surprised (but what could really surprise him anymore?), he walked in.

He first noticed the height up to the windows. They were at least seven feet from the floor. He pondered that for a moment, then remembered the religious wars that had torn the country apart in centuries past. If you needed to take refuge in a church (and where else?), you would be safer to have higher walls than lower windows. Under the windows were bas reliefs of people in fancy clothes with names above them. Some kind of memorials, he wondered? As he walked into the church, he saw some also as part of the floor. Graves! People were buried here in the church!

"I'm sure not in Kansas anymore!" He muttered to himself. He admired the carvings around the altar and on the pulpit, and sat for a while. The silence was profound. He didn't realize he'd fallen asleep until he woke up with a start when he heard a door shut.

He got up, rather sheepishly, and walked back to the door, passing an older man who had obviously been the one who had come in and shut the door. The man was making the sign of the cross as Sam passed him with a nod.

Sam had walked a few times around a tiny garden space beside the main street before he really saw that there were some kind of markers in it. He went to look at them more closely.

"Kreigsmarker," said one at the top. 'War Marker,' Sam told himself. He later learned this marker was not so much to honor the dead, but to admonish the living for causing their deaths. When you lose a war, the entire perspective is different. On each side of the heading was an Iron Cross, the German symbol during the Great War. Below that heading was a list of names. Idly, he scanned down the list, you always look for your family name.

"Gantz!" There it was. "Pankratz Gantz." He was puzzled. Wheels began to turn in Sam's brain. Something about that odd name was familiar. "Oh, my God!" He gasped. That was the brother of his great grandfather who was killed in the Kaiser's War. "Oh. My. GOD!!!" He involuntarily stepped back from the marker as if he had been hit. He had to get a better perspective on this knowledge. How could it be here?? What did this mean???

He was HOME!!!

This was the original family village. No wonder the name sounded somewhat familiar. He hadn't actually remembered it, but in the back of his brain, it was there. He must have heard it when he was a very little child and older ones in the family talked about it. The family had moved away and no one had been back, interest had died out. Now, he had been brought back.

Sam sank to the ground crying. Feelings of relief poured over him. Somehow he had come back. He suddenly felt he BELONGED here! This was his village! His ancestors had been here for generations, lived here, died here where he was now. It was overwhelming.

Sam simply sat and took in this new realization of where he was and a new awareness of who he was.

'The cemetery,' he thought. 'I need to see if there are any family graves here. There must be. He got up and walked back to the cemetery. This time, he walked in the gate and began carefully looking at the names on the stones. He was startled to see a list of names on each stone, each name with it's own dates. That didn't make any sense. Then he began to notice the sequence of the dates. The oldest dates were at the top of the stone with newer and newer dates going down. On some stones, the last names were the same, on others there was a mix of one name with others, and yet on other stones the names were all different, but in each case the dates became more and more recent the further down the stone they went.

Sam was confused. Why were all these names on each of the graves. That didn't make sense. Then, suddenly, there was a grave with "Gantz" on it. All the names on the stone, but one in the middle, were Gantz. Here was a list of his family! He didn't recognize any of the first names, but that didn't matter. There had to be a connection. The next stone had some Gantz names mixed with other names. Sam shook his head in bewilderment. But there were no dates beside any Gantz name after Hitler's war.

"I need to find someone to explain this to me," he said aloud to himself. "Who might know English in this town? I can ask at the Gasthaus, they should know someone who knows English. At least the woman should, since her son is in the states. He was glad he'd brought his English/German dictionary. He was going to need it to construct the sentences to ask why there were so many names on each grave stone.

Back in his room, he set out to write out the sentences he would need: Who can speak English? Why are many names on each grave stone? And others.

His sentences worked. It took a couple of days, but Sam was directed to a teacher at the local school, where English was taught as a mandatory course. He learned that all the names on each stone were the names of all the people buried in that single grave. Bodies were not embalmed, but were buried quickly after death, in plain wooden coffins. Natural decomposition was let to do its work. Each grave was rented from the village for a period of twenty years. If anyone in the family who was renting the grave died in that time, they could be buried in that same grave. What bones had not decomposed since the last burial were put in the Knochenhaus, a small structure at the back of the cemetery. Few bones survived decomposition. The cemetery never needed to be expanded.

Sam took down all the names and dates on any stone with his family name. Other names on those stones could be women of the family who took a new name when they married and, for some reason, were buried here. He took note of those names and dates on other stones too. He wasn't sure how they might all be connected, but in such a small village, there was very likely some connection. He'd never had time for family history before, now he had plenty of that!

He found a purpose in writing all this down that felt deeper than any business deal he had ever made, no matter the amount of money he's gained by them. This work was real, it was a part of him, a part of his life, a part of who he was.

He would look up the names, find out how they were connected to him. How could they not be? Gantz was not exactly a common name at home, but here? He didn't know. This discovery was amazing.

Other days, Sam hiked the forest in the hills. There were well-marked hiking trails, mostly lumber roads. It was a managed forest. Logging was done on a careful basis so that younger trees were given space to grow. The harvested logs were marked with the date of its being cut down on the butt end. Sam was sure there was an inventory noting each log. Germans were such good record keepers. Sunlight streamed through the canopy of the trees. Birds flew about. It looked like a fairyland forest. He almost expected to see a castle appear around the next bend. But there was none. This wasn't a movie.

One day Sam mentioned his curiosity about nearby castles to his landlady and she said there had been a castle in the village, but it had burned over a century earlier and was never rebuilt. Its stones were used for new houses in the village. There was an ancient hill castle in the forest, and she pointed out the door to the peak of the hill where it was located.

The next day, Sam went looking and found it. Not much was left. At the top of the hill was a space inside a ring of earth that looked as if it had been dug up repeatedly, and it may well have been. Several feet down the hill from that ring of earth was another ring of earth all around the hill, and another lower than that. The rings were obviously man-made and defensive in nature. Sam wondered if one or more of those rings had had a wooden palisade.

Not far from the outermost ring, he noticed a line of stones that were similar in size and shape. There were two lines actually, and parallel. The stones were all oval shaped, lying long ways, and on the top of each was carved a straight line. Sam knew these could not have naturally occurred, one, maybe, but not two rows of them lined parallel along the side of this hill with the fort. The distance between the lines of stones was about the width of a one-lane road. The stones had to mark a road! Why else would they be there?

Back at the Gasthaus, he asked about the stones.

"Roman Strasse," he was told, a Roman street or road.

This was central Franconia, or Franken. Sam had no idea Roman influence had spread this far north and east. He was impressed. Even if his family hadn't been here in Roman times, and who knew if they had or not, he was amazed at this connection.

This trip had deepened Sam's understanding of his identity, who he was, where he had come from. He had never expected this to happen from this trip. He was connected, truly and deeply connected to a place. It had a history, HE now had a history. Sam felt complete and whole at a deeper level than he had ever imagined possible. He had found his long-ago home, a place that gave his identity. He was deeply satisfied. He had found a whole new, more complete self.

And, he had found his home!

SQUEAK, PRINCE OF THE SERENGETI
Katherine Pritchett

I am Squeak, African lion, Prince of the Serengeti. I stretch leisurely from my nap atop a warm flat rock. The lionesses have brought down an eland, and I saunter toward them to eat my fill. What's this? My dad just swatted me. Ow, that hurt! Why is he pushing me away from lunch? I see my brother running away from the pride. When Dad hits me again, I join my brother, but he snarls a non-welcome to me.

It's okay. I'm a lion; I'll just get my own dinner. I stalk a baby elephant, like the apex predator I am. Hold on, her mom is running at me and sends me rolling with a swipe of her trunk. I know where I'm not wanted.

I'll hunt a zebra instead. Tenderer meat anyway. I have to be very quiet to creep though the tall grass to get close to a fat tender stripey. Ow! This one's pal kicked me in the ribs. I roll over and over to get away.

Now I'm hungry and thirsty. I'll get a drink of water. But as I'm lapping away, a crocodile glides my way. I jump back to the dry ground just as those big jaws snap shut.

Just then a crack of thunder signals incoming lightning. Wow! That was close. My fur is still standing on end when the rain starts. It's cold! Soon, hail starts. The pellets keep getting bigger as I run for a cave nearby. I'm met with angry growls. Hyenas have taken cover there. I cower under a small outcropping, with lightning striking all too close.

Thunder continues, roaring like my father. Suddenly, as I wake, I feel my human's hand stroking my fur. I purr and snuggle closer to her. She feeds me the kibble I like, brushes me, keeps fresh water out for me and gives me toys. She talks to me and calls me "Baby Cat." She saved me from the outdoors and nursed me to health. I'm inside where it's never too hot or too cold. It's dry and I am safe. I think it's better to be a house cat than a wild lion.

DARKNESS
Elie Stone

You call to the darkness in me

I love this about you
It was so comforting
To not be alone there

In the dark

To have a hand
To hold

To face the things
I wanted to hide

From myself
Others

…the world

You gave me courage
To peak through timid fingers

…then more bravely
Evaluate fully

Bringing those parts of me
Into the light
Integrating those pieces
Previously rejected

The darkness is still there

I visit

Yet I chose to live in the light
Where you aren't ready
To go

So I must say goodbye

For now

I hope that the light in me
Will call to the light in you
…when you are ready
Step out of the shadows

There I will be
Hand outstretched
Welcoming you

Into the light

POTENTIAL
Elie Stone

I envision so much potential
Vivid images of how we could be
Flooding my mind
A home
Love, passion, laughter
Adventures
New experiences

Potential -
A dangerous thing
We can pour in all of our hopes
Our dreams
Its tantalizing promises

Promises,
Seductive and sweet
Curling around us
Dark smoke tendrils
Rippling along our skin
Feeling so real
Overwhelming our senses

Almost tangible

A false foundation to build upon
Luring us into a sense of tomorrow
One which may never come

For but a gentle breeze
Could blow it away

Ravaging the beauty
We built in our minds

Leaving
Only
This moment

So I offer you all of my now's
The only thing I truly have to give
Pouring my heart and soul
Into each
As if it was my last
They are all yours

As am I

Excerpt from

RECOGNIZING GOD'S HAND IN MY LIFE
Laura Wright

My parents divorced when I was five. This life-changing event colored my worldview and what I believed about myself.

I am the youngest of three children, having two older brothers. My mom dated my stepdad for three years before asking her to marry him. He was 20 years her senior and a deacon at First Baptist Church in a neighboring town. His children were already adults, so he was experiencing a new set of teens and pre-teens later in life. It would have been challenging for anyone. The greatest thing I learned from his example was commitment. Neither ever threatened divorce, even though they endured some tough times.

I attended First Baptist the summer before beginning 3rd grade until I was 15. During the summer of that last year, I heard Pastor McIlvene preach a Sunday message that you could accept Jesus as your Savior and not worry about how you lived your life. So, I walked the aisle for a free ticket to live my life any way I wanted and still get to heaven.

[Pro 14:12 AMP] 12 There is a way which seems right to a man and appears straight before him, But its end is the way of death.

Keith was a boy I had seen around at church and in school. We began dating that summer, and life at home was difficult. Mom and my stepdad had welcomed a

84

new daughter, and I was in the way. I felt unwanted and unloved. Keith and I had a typical teen dating experience of on-again, off-again. A few weeks later, after a break-up with Keith and a rebellious bout with my parents, I moved back to my hometown of San Augustine with my biological father.

My dad was in a relationship with another woman and worked all the time. He was only in town on the weekends. His girlfriend already had three younger girls and resented a teenager full of angst living in her house. We did not get along and were in competition for the little time my dad was home. After one last big fight, she insisted I move out.

During tenth grade, I lived alone in a 15-foot travel trailer about 8 miles outside town. My dad would come once a week and take me grocery shopping. It was one of the most peaceful times in my life. I read and listened to the few cassette tapes I owned on a stereo Dad gave me for Christmas. Somehow, Keith found out where I lived. One Saturday in early winter, he showed up unexpectedly and we resumed our dating relationship.

My next-door neighbor worked at the courthouse. Since I was a troubled teen living alone, I was forced to move in with my maternal grandmother by April, at least until the end of the school year.

Then, that summer, my mom and my stepdad got me to move back to Lufkin. I stayed with them over the summer, but things were not better. Before school started, I moved in with Keith's paternal grandmother,

Nanny. I lived with her until Keith and I were married in December of my senior year.

My experience with church was backbiting, and social elitists focused on popularity and control. So, after the wedding, I was done with church and all the hypocritical, judgmental people. I was looking to belong somewhere and be accepted and cared for, and I never got that from church people. As soon as we were married, I left the church behind and never cared to go back.

My life took a deep downward turn.   I did whatever I pleased and allowed my emotions to rule my life. I was depressed. All of the sins I practiced brought me no satisfaction or lasting pleasure. It made me feel alone, even with Keith. I felt lost and afraid of being rejected by others. My self-worth plummeted.

[Jas 4:1-4 AMP] 1 What leads to [the unending] quarrels and conflicts among you? Do they not come from your [hedonistic] desires that wage war in your [bodily] members [fighting for control over you]? 2 You are jealous and covet [what others have] and your lust goes unfulfilled; so you murder. You are envious and cannot obtain [the object of your envy]; so you fight and battle. You do not have because you do not ask [it of God]. 3 You ask [God for something] and do not receive it, because you ask with wrong motives [out of selfishness or with an unrighteous agenda], so that [when you get what you want] you may spend it on your [hedonistic] desires. 4 You adulteresses [disloyal sinners--flirting with the world and breaking your vow to God]! Do you not know that being the world's friend [that is, loving the things of the world] is being God's enemy? So whoever chooses to be a friend of the world makes himself an enemy of God.

Five years later, Keith and I had two children. We lived in Abilene, and both worked long hours. We never saw one another except in passing. I began to listen to bad influences at work and was tired of how things were. I was jealous of people's nice houses and their seemingly unfettered life. I was in the middle of another flirtatious affair, ready to be free of all responsibilities. None of these things made me a new and better person. Now, I was depressed and suicidal. It was no surprise when Keith and I separated, and he filed for divorce.

[Rev 3:17 AMP] 17 'Because you say, "I am rich, and have prospered and grown wealthy, and have need of nothing," and you do not know that you are wretched and miserable and poor and blind and naked [without hope and in great need].

How could I rescue myself from such a downward spiral? I then realized that I had made a huge mistake. It was costing me my only connected relationship. Keith mercifully invited me over for dinner a few months into the separation. It was his birthday and he shared how my actions had wounded him. I stayed the night and made the phone call two months later, "Guess what? We're pregnant."

The state of Texas won't go through with a divorce if the woman is pregnant- you must wait until the baby is born. And in our case, for paternity testing.

[Psa 127:3-5 AMP] 3 Behold, children are a heritage and gift from the LORD, The fruit of the womb a reward. 4 Like arrows in the hand of a warrior, So are the children of one's youth. 5 How blessed [happy and fortunate] is the man whose quiver is filled with them; They will not be ashamed When they speak with their enemies [in gatherings] at the [city] gate.

Our third child, a son, was born in February. Keith couldn't decide whether to stay married or proceed with the divorce. Spending time with me, his heart desired to reclaim our vows, but then he visited his parents and chose to proceed with divorce. Finally, he took a temporary duty assignment to Panama for three months. The children and I lived in base housing.

One Saturday, while he was gone, I had a most unusual sense (that I now see was the Holy Spirit of God) urging me to get ready for church the following day. This was rather comical. I usually don't have thoughts like this. For the past five years, I had not thought about church, religion, or anything of the sort. I didn't own a Bible or consider myself religious in any way. However, I didn't even think about it. I cleaned, set the table for breakfast, bathed the kids, and washed their hair. I put them to bed at a decent hour and set my alarm. Early the next morning, we got up and got dressed. We ate breakfast and got in the car. This was no small task with three small children, two in car seats and diapers, but I certainly wasn't about to disobey my clear instructions from above.

Amazingly, it wasn't until I had the car cranked and ready to put it in drive that I realized I had no idea where a church was, when it would start, or even know anyone else who attended church. But that didn't matter. Such was my determination to obey. I turned the car off and sat there crying for a moment. Then I cried to the One who hears us, the One who had given me such clear instruction to get ready, "God, I don't know where to go or who to call." [Mat 6:8 AMP] 8 "So do not be like them [praying as they do]; for your Father knows what you need before you ask Him."

That's when He reminded me of my coworkers at the pizza company. Two of them attended church, so in a call or two, I knew where and when to go. It was 7 a.m. The church would not open for some time. In my earnestness, we drove over and parked in the empty lot, waiting for people to show up. Once a few cars were in the parking lot, I got out and took the kids to the nursery and Sunday School.

I sat in the back, purposefully close to the aisle. At churches I attended years back, there would be an altar call near the end of services. It was a time for those who felt moved to respond to God's call. I only needed to wait through the entire service, which I paid little attention to, for the invitation. I was impatient and tapping my foot. I knew I   had nothing to offer. I was very aware of my failures, shortcomings, and sins. I needed God for an honest and lasting change. I had already tried everything on my own and was left empty and hurt. Jesus was the only Way and Truth to a new Life. When the first notes rang out from the piano, I rushed to the front, dropped to my knees, and cried out with tears flowing freely down my cheeks, "God, I have nothing to offer You, but all that I am and all that I have is Yours."

[2Co 5:17 AMP] 17 Therefore if anyone is in Christ [that is, grafted in, joined to Him by faith in Him as Savior], he is a new creature [reborn and renewed by the Holy Spirit]; the old things [the previous moral and spiritual condition] have passed away. Behold, new things have come [because spiritual awakening brings a new life].

Immediately, I was changed before God by the power of Jesus. I felt peace. My spirit and soul were changed, and ultimately, my life and body were also changed. My life was full of everything BUT Godly living when I stepped forward. However, in short order, my outward lifestyle reflected the new me. I avoided those self-destructive temptations and began a life of Bible study, disciplined prayer, and changed habits. I now understand the requirements for lasting change and its great benefits.

I clearly know that God took me step-by-step, teaching me about His Word and His Ways. He provided everything I needed, and He still does. He completely transformed me- my wardrobe, my habits, my words, my reactions. [2Th 2:13 AMP] 13 But we should and are [morally] obligated [as debtors] always to give thanks to God for you, believers beloved by the Lord, because God has chosen you from the beginning for salvation through the sanctifying work of the Spirit [that sets you apart for God's purpose] and by your faith in the truth [of God's word that leads you to spiritual maturity].

The new changes included a restored marriage relationship that has grown even stronger year by year. Family relationships I previously had destroyed through a self-absorbed mindset and activities and were restored in ways I never could have imagined. He also redeemed the years I wasted on selfish desires and empty habits.

[1Co 1:27-28 AMP] 27 But God has selected [for His purpose] the foolish things of the world to shame the wise [revealing their ignorance], and God has selected [for His purpose] the weak things of the world to shame the things which are strong [revealing their frailty]. 28 God has selected [for His purpose] the insignificant (base) things of the world, and the things that are despised and treated with contempt, [even] the things that are nothing, so that He might reduce to nothing the things that are.

[Rom 4:7-8 AMP] 7 "BLESSED and HAPPY and FAVORED ARE THOSE WHOSE LAWLESS ACTS HAVE BEEN FORGIVEN, AND WHOSE SINS HAVE BEEN COVERED UP and COMPLETELY BURIED. 8 "BLESSED and HAPPY and FAVORED IS THE MAN WHOSE SIN THE LORD WILL NOT TAKE INTO ACCOUNT nor CHARGE AGAINST HIM."

He personally taught me His Word and what it means to believe in Him. What it means to walk by faith. [Job 19:25-27 AMP] 25 "For I know that my Redeemer and Vindicator lives, And at the last He will take His stand upon the earth. 26 "Even after my [mortal] skin is destroyed [by death], Yet from my [immortal] flesh I will see God, 27 Whom I, even I, will see for myself,

And my eyes will see Him and not another! My heart faints within me. "

Job 19 (AMP) Blue Letter Bible. Accessed 16 Aug, 2024.
https://www.blueletterbible.org/amp/job/19/1/s_455001

[Job 19:25 NASB95] 25 "As for me, I know that my Redeemer lives, And at the last He will take His stand on the earth.

Made in United States
North Haven, CT
03 October 2024

58205043R00052